FROM *Santa* WITH LOVE

ALEXANDER BABAYAN

Second edition 2024

ISBN 979-8-9892452-1-5
Ebook ISBN 979-8-9892452-0-8

To Mom and Dad who gave us many happy Christmases.
Requiem aeternam dona eis, Domine,
et lux perpetua luceat eis.

Contents

1. Breaking up is hard to do   1

2. Work as usual   6

3. A night at the bar   12

4. Happy Thanksgiving   19

5. It's December, let's meet strangers   29

6. The plot thickens   36

7. I thought about Mary   45

8. Let's get Merry and Bright   56

9. Old friends to the rescue   61

10. Don't panic, Santa Claus is in town   70

11. Get real, fast   77

12. Christmas Party   86

13. After Party   98

14. Merry Christmas   107

15. Conclusion, give or take   125

Breaking up is hard to do

Anthony and Mary sit at a table in their favorite restaurant, the kind of place where candles burn longer than the dream of everlasting love. It's an August night in New York and Anthony feels the cool breeze from the window gently brush his face. From inside they can see how the leaves twirl and twist in a delicate dance with the wind. Seated at the round table, the waitress hands them the menu and leaves. Under the soft glow of the white candle, he watches Mary tackle the menu, flipping through the pages like an absent-minded professor searching for a formula. He smiles and stares at his menu, but his mind is elsewhere – more precisely, on Christmas Eve. He has a special plan: the perfect proposal under his parents' tree, down on one knee and with any luck, a gentle snowfall. He imagines holding Mary's trembling hand, slipping the ring on her finger, and professing his undying love. Mary, on the other hand, appears to be creating her own ice storm. She seems to be more distant than a spaceship drifting through the void of space. Anthony had noticed it lately but dismissed it as exhaustion from her demanding job as a trauma nurse.

"Is the food, okay?" Anthony asks, trying not to sound too serious. Mary jumps straight to the point: "Tony, are you happy?" Anthony feels the heaviness of the question. It's like a grenade going to explode any moment. He wonders why wouldn't he be happy? While trying to maintain his calm he replies: "With you, I am." At the same time reaching for her hand. Mary gently pulls back her hand and says: "We need to talk." The four dreaded words that make any man shudder. Anthony knows exactly what it means. He sighs, trying to be calm and says: "Okay... about what?"

"About our relationship," she starts, her eyes hollow "You know I'm very fond of you Tony, but we are not soulmates."

Anthony quickly replies: "What do you mean we're not soulmates? I love you!" He suddenly digests her words and trying not to yell continues: "Fond of me?! What the heck is that supposed to mean? You don't love me?"

Mary winces: "This is really difficult for me-" Anthony cuts her off. "Difficult for you?! You're about to dump me, and it's difficult for you!" Then continues with sarcasm: "I am so very sorry for your pain!"

"Tony, please don't be like that. Let me explain. I've met someone." Anthony shakes his head in disbelief. "Wait, it's not like that. I haven't cheated on you," she insists quickly. "It's just that I've fallen in love with someone else. I feel like we're soulmates."

Anthony twists in pain. "How, can you do this to me?" His voice broken. "I still care for you," Mary says, her voice trembling. "But we are not soulmates. I can't help it. Gary's on my mind day and night. He's the one I've fallen in love with. It's not fair to string you along when I know there's no future for us. I'm sorry Tony. I didn't plan it this way. It just happened. But it was love at first sight. I know it's hard for you to hear." Anthony is crushed under those words. They sit in silence in the restaurant's ambient noise. Then she says: "I will go back to my apartment tonight. If it's okay, I'll come later and pick up my things."

"Sure, come by anytime. I don't get to have a saying in this, am I?" Anthony replies sarcastically. Mary gives him a sad smile. "Do you want to finish your meal?"

He scoffs: "Yeah, let's have two steaks. I've worked up quite the appetite."

"Don't be bitter, Tony," she pleads. "I don't want us to separate like this."

Anthony thinks, *I don't want us to separate at all*. But he swallows those words.

Later, parked outside her apartment complex, Mary gently touches his face, then leans in and gives him a kiss on the cheek. "I'm so sorry Tony. I hope you find your soulmate someday." As she walks away, he thinks *I'm already losing the love of my life*. He never saw it coming. For Anthony everything was perfect. He was picturing their wedding and their life together. How could he be so wrong? It felt like a sucker-punch straight to the gut.

Reaching to silence the alarm, Anthony glances at the date. *It's official*, he thinks, *November 1*. He is in the timeframe for Christmas. Ever since his childhood, Anthony considered November 1 as the beginning of the Christmas season. It was time to start planning on choosing the right presents. Sure, as a child, he would want every new toy that would come to market throughout the year. But only from November 1 would he give serious thought about which toy he wanted the most. That specific toy would be the subject of his letter to Santa. The rest of the things could come from Mom, Dad, aunties, uncles, and grandparents. Anything he could get from them would be fine. But that one particular present would be the most important one. The one that he would really ... really

... really, wish for! Come December 1, he would write his letter to Santa and ask for that most important gift. Everyone knows that only one letter can be sent to Santa, and whatever you ask for in that letter will be what Santa brings. Once it's written and posted, there's no going back. No changes or revisions. So, it was important to think it through before writing and sending a letter to Santa. That's why Anthony needed a lot of thinking and soul-searching before sending his letter. However, like most of us, as time went by and Anthony grew older, he stopped believing in Santa. After all, Santa was for bringing toys, and toys were for kids. So, eventually he gave up on Santa and the letters, but this one weird quirk of his remained.

November 1 is the beginning of planning what he wanted the most for Christmas. With or without Santa, he would try hard to plan for the best Christmas ever. He has a system for it. First, he saves money all year long. Then, starting in December, he gives half of the savings to his choice of charities and meal centers. Of the other half, two-thirds are spent on gifts and presents for family and friends, and the rest is used for decorations, taking his buddies out, and going to a few of the season's events. That is his usual annual ritual. But this year, it's different.

Looking at the clock, he doesn't smile or feel giddy in his heart. He doesn't jump out of bed with childlike excitement. This year, his heart is heavy. To be honest, this year he isn't that keen on Christmas. Anthony is thirty-two years old, with no hope of a meaningful future. His definition of a meaningful future is having a family—a wife, maybe a couple of children, and hopefully, many grandchildren. He doesn't see any of these things happening and feels like all hope is lost.

The reason for this despair is the last breakup. Another one of many. He's stuck in a dating loop. Every year he dates a woman, and after a few months they go their separate ways. Nothing is stable, nothing is reliable. Women often think that men do not worry about things like relationship, family, stability, and reliability. But they do. Men *do* feel those things and want them. This last relationship was important to Anthony. He and Mimi (that's his nickname for Mary) were in a relationship for over a year, and he believed it was the real deal. He began calling her Mimi on their second date. While she was a bit annoyed, she accepted it. Right then and there, he knew she must like him a lot to let him give her a nickname so soon. He started having deeper feelings for her and eventually they fell in love. In his heart, Anthony knew she was the one. However, sometimes Fate has other plans which usually don't go with our plans. He is still living in the twilight zone of that date. He still vividly remembers every word that came out of her mouth. Like a broken record, it keeps playing in his mind: *I still care for you very much ... we are not soulmates ... I met someone else ... Gary is in my mind day and night ... I've fallen in love with ... we are soulmates ... I'm sorry Tony.*

For the past three months, he has been living and acting like a ghost, as if nothing inside is alive. He works, breathes, eats, and sleeps, but he's not living. This gloomy and cold November morning is no different. It's getting colder, especially in the mornings. As he gets up to go about his morning business, he thinks to himself, *November has arrived and now I have to scratch my plans.* He had planned a beautiful proposal for Mimi. They were going to spend Christmas with his parents. He was going to ask for her hand in marriage on Christmas Eve in the backyard of the home he grew up in—right under his favorite tree—that tall, beautiful red maple Dad planted when they bought the house. He grew up spending many hours under its shade. This year, he had decided that was the most important thing he'd want for Christmas. But now everything has changed. The plan is gone, and along with it, Anthony's enthusiasm and excitement for Christmas.

Work as usual

A nthony is a senior engineer at a software development company and is working on an experimental AI application. He loves his job and the project. But lately, he doesn't feel like working anymore. His head is somewhere else, and he's beginning to lag on deadlines. He's been working at this company for eight years, and they know him to be responsible and punctual with his deadlines. He is a model employee. Up until now. His manager knows about his situation and tries to be patient with him. But her patience has limits, and she doesn't know how to get him out of this situation.

With the company closing in December and the holiday shutdowns, things become more hectic. They need to meet their project milestone before the end of the year. To get him out of his shell, his manager, Lindsey, decided to give him a side project to clear his mind. She put him in charge of the department's Christmas party. She knows how Anthony takes Christmas planning seriously and thought it would put him in his element. Maybe the distraction would help him get back on his project and reach the milestone on time. Anthony didn't like the idea at first, but his friends suggested it would be worth trying. After all, taking him out bar hopping and picking up girls didn't seem to work.

Though they mostly worked from home, his team had decided to go to the office one day a week. He usually starts his day at seven-thirty. He walks to his desk and turns on his laptop computer, noticing he has a message from his manager.

Lindsey: "GM, it's Nov 1st!"

Anthony: "???"

Lindsey: "Your plans for the Christmas party! You should be starting to work on that."

Anthony: "I thought you already forgot, and I could get away with not doing it."

Lindsey: "Come on Tony, you said you'll do it. We need a party. It's Christmas!"

Anthony: "La-di-da!"

Lindsey: "What's with the humbug attitude? You were never like that!"

Anthony: "You know very well what's with it."

Lindsey: "That's why you need a distraction."

Anthony: "I have this deadline."

Lindsey: "Which isn't getting anywhere."

Anthony: "I know I'm a bit late, but I'm on top of it."

Lindsey: "Well, while you're napping on top of it, plan our PARTY!!"

Ouch, Anthony thinks to himself. *Am I really that behind?* He knows Lindsey means well and is only trying to help him. *Okay, I'll do it.*

Anthony: "Where should I start?"

Lindsey: "Coordinate with Jasmine. She has done this every year and knows where to start. You can ask her to help you. Just don't take all of my assistant's time."

Anthony: "Oookay!"

Jasmine usually starts her day at eight o'clock. Anthony likes to start a bit earlier to get some work done before others come in. Lindsey is always in the office or online around seven o'clock. He goes to his coffee machine and starts his daily double espresso before coming back to his project. *Yup, I'm behind alright.* He decides to focus on the tasks and try to bring them to date as much as possible. He looks out the window. The weather was getting cold. The mornings are cloudy and gray. He never minded it before, since it was a sign of being closer to Christmas. He loved Christmas because of the joy they had at home. His parents would go to great lengths to make the holiday as joyful and happy for the children as possible. Even during difficult times, his parents did their best to keep everyone happy. But this year, looking out the window only made him gloomier. It seems that in times of joy, we often remember the good times, and in times of sorrow, we think of the difficult times of our lives. That's what's happening to Anthony. As he is looking outside the window, the gray sky brings back memories of the time when his father was out of work.

He and his sisters were still too young to understand the severity of their situation. There were some days they didn't have anything to eat other than bread and water, but their parents did their best to keep them happy. That Christmas, although they couldn't afford anything, the kids insisted on a tree, and after a lot of soul-searching and number-crunching, Mom and Dad took them to the tree lot. It was late, and the owner was preparing to close for the day. They checked the prices on different trees and picked one that was close to the amount of money they had. The kids liked it. Realizing they didn't have quite enough money for the tree, Dad went to the owner and explained the situation and asked for a discount. The owner wasn't very keen on it at first, but one look at the kids and he took their money and let them have the tree. Dad was so happy he leaped forward, hugged the owner tight, and gave him a big kiss on his cheek. The poor man was stunned and just stood there. Mom and the kids started laughing, and then Dad and the owner joined in the laughter. A painful tree buying event turned into a happy and funny moment. That Christmas, everyone was happy and grateful for being able to afford a tree. There weren't any presents from Mom and Dad, but something for each of them from Santa. Years later, Anthony guessed the presents most likely must have been from a local charity. Their church had a similar program. His family often reminisced about that night during Christmas.

He pushes those memories back and focuses on his project. He is immersed in his work when a ding from his messenger grabs his attention. It's Jasmine. He looks at the clock on the laptop—it's nine-thirty. Almost two hours of uninterrupted work! He's pleased with himself and happy the work took his mind off of the breakup for a brief time.

Jasmine: "Lindsey told me you will handle the Christmas party. Lemme know if you need help."

Anthony: "AAMOF, I need to know where to begin. I was thinking of having the party at the office."

Jasmine: "Up to you. But this year we have a bigger budget, and we haven't had a decent party for the past couple of years. It would be nice to have the party at a venue."

Anthony: "We have a budget?"

Jasmine: "Man, you really need help ... lol"

Anthony: "LOL"

Jasmine: "Yes, we have a budget. You didn't ask Lindsey?"

Anthony: "I wasn't even sure if I was going to do this!"

Jasmine: "No worries. We have enough money to have a party for 200 ppl in a top venue. You wanna choose the place, or should I find something for you?"

Anthony: "Why do I have the feeling that it's going to be your way?"

Jasmine: "cuz you're intelligent and smart."

Anthony: "I tell you what, you give me the top three places and we'll choose one together."

Jasmine: "On it."

So far, so good, he thought. He didn't need to tire himself over this. The smart thing was to let Jasmine take care of it. He knows it's kind of cheating, but is hoping it will work out. Ten minutes later, his messenger dings again. It's Lindsey.

Lindsey: "I told you don't take all her time! You're supposed to do this on your own and get help when you needed."

Anthony: "I needed"

Lindsey: "Don't give me that. Googling a few venues and choosing one doesn't need help. You can't get out of this one that easy."

Anthony: "Ok, I'll do the rest myself."

Now that the matter of the Christmas party is settled, it's time to get back to his project. Again, he looks out the window at the gray, cloudy sky. He remembers how, before the breakup, he and Mary used to like these November mornings. One of the good things about Christmas is that it brings cheer to a gloomy winter. Winter is a time of hibernation when nature goes into resting. While most animals learn to live with the pace of seasons and the rotation of Earth around the Sun, we humans are somehow the opposite. We incline towards being busy at all times—hence the saying that idle hands are the devil's workshop. For the fast-paced human, winter becomes very boring. If we don't do positive work, we are going to get up to mischief. Who knows? Maybe most of the wars in history were devised and planned during winter time. That's probably why Christmas becomes a favorite time of the year. In the middle of a slowing nature, we tend to celebrate and get busy with helping each other, giving gifts, and trying to enjoy our time by attending parties and events. We go out more, and even manage to enjoy the cold and slushy snow. Anthony feels he isn't in the mood for work anymore. One look at his laptop and he changes his mind. The project has to get up to date. He snaps out of his thoughts and forces himself to get busy. That's another human ability. We can force ourselves to do many things when we put our minds to it.

A night at the bar

Anthony has a group of friends here in New York. They've been friends since college. When he moved to New York, they were his roommates and classmates, and they kept in touch after graduation. After all these years, they're still friends. Although one is married and the other two have girlfriends, they still find time to get together now and then. When Anthony was with Mary, they would all go out together. They also have a poker night once a month. However, poker had been postponed after the breakup, and his friends made more effort to take him out and not let him be alone for a long time during this difficult time. If they couldn't be with him, they would text him. After all, that's what good friends do. They support each other in times of need. A couple of days later, the three decide to take Anthony out. After exchanging a few text messages, the time and place are set.

That afternoon, after work, Anthony gets ready for the night with the boys. He decides to take the public transit since they'll be drinking. It's a half-hour ride, and he has plenty of time. He is grateful that his friends are keeping him company. They know how he loves Christmastime, and want to cheer him up. When he gets there, his friends are already waiting.

Alec waves to him, letting him know they are there. He walks over and says hi.

"Hey guys. You're quick."

"Hey, let's go in," Alec responds.

Jimmy, another one of his friends, speaks up. "If they don't have a table, see if we can sit at the counter."

"Forget the table. If there's room at the counter, let's just go there," Ben chimes in.

They go in and there isn't enough room at the bar, so they ask for a table. Luckily, there's one available, and they're seated. They look at the menu and start with their drinks. Jimmy turns to the waiter and asks, "Can we have a pitcher?"

"I need something stronger than beer," Anthony says.

"Make it a boilermaker," Jimmy says.

"Hmm ... I meant something like Bloody Mary."

The guys roll their eyes.

"Here we go. Not even two minutes and Mary has to come up in the conversation," Ben says. They all start laughing. Anthony made that comment on purpose, knowing they would be annoyed.

"Come on guys, let him wallow in his sorrow," Alec says.

"What sorrow? People breakup all the time," Ben replies.

"I feel sad," Anthony states.

"Shut up," Alec says before turning to the waiter. "He'll have a shot of whiskey, and we're going to have a pitcher. Thank you."

"Coming right up. I'll give you some time to decide on your food," the waiter replies, and leaves.

Turning to Ben, Anthony asks, "How's the business?"

"The store is doing okay. As usual, this is the time we make the most money of the year."

"Do people still buy books?"

"Do you?"

"Uh, every now and then. I think people mostly buy eBooks, and even if they want a print copy, there's Amazon. How do you guys compete with them?"

"That's the challenge. I'm busy modernizing the store. We got new inventory, offer more services, and have a plan to expand."

"What kind of services are there in a bookstore?"

"Plenty dude. I didn't get my MBA for nothing."

Jimmy interrupts Ben and Anthony's conversation, and says, "You got your MBA?!" They laugh at the comment, because back in college, Ben was the party boy. He spent less time in classes than he did at frat parties, chugging beer. To everyone's surprise, he took over his father's bookstore business, and he was the first to marry. His friends were amazed how he turned into a very responsible family man. He's been married for six years now and has a daughter. He met Lucy in the bookstore and they've been happily married ever since. "You were saying," Anthony turns back to Ben, resuming their conversation.

"Well, there are book readings and classes. We have cooking classes where we offer customers a chance to try recipes they read in a book. This encourages them to buy the cookbook and have hands-on experience. There's also tutoring classes for kids. We hire a teacher to have thirty-minute sessions on school subjects like Math, Literature, and History."

"Isn't that costly? Do you even make any profit?" Alec asked.

"Not if we're doing it in small quantities," Ben replied. "We also sell our books on Amazon, so that takes care of delivery. We broadcast our classes on YouTube and our customers get to watch those videos. All of that generates income. Companies like Amazon don't do these things."

"Interesting! If you think about it, there's plenty that mom-and-pop stores can do to stay in business. They just have to make use of the new technology, like social media and the internet," Alec said.

"Exactly. That's what we're trying to do. With our store modernized, we create a great atmosphere for customers to come in and enjoy their time," Ben continues. "We offer many more services. For example, during the holiday season, we offer gift wrapping."

"That, most places offer," Alec says.

"Yes, but they do a sloppy job. We offer a professional gift-wrapping service. We have customers who bring their gifts and ask us to wrap them. We charge them for that, which is another source of income."

"So, you did pay attention to those classes you didn't attend," Jimmy pipes in. Again, everybody laughs.

"You were with me half the time."

"Yeah, but only half. Lord knows what was going on the other half that I wasn't there!"

Their conversation pauses as the waiter returns and takes their orders. As the waiter walks away, Alec turns to Tony.

"Hey Tony, how's your project coming along? You mentioned you have some artificial intelligence project thingy."

"He doesn't have enough intelligence, so he's making some artificial ones for himself," Jimmy interjects, much to the amusement of their friends. Jimmy has always been the joker of the group. Ben is relieved that the attention has shifted from him, and joins the laughter.

"I was behind, but the past few weeks I submerged myself in the work, and now it's going well. You know, I'm glad we're working from home. If this would have happened when we were going to the office, I don't know how I could bear it."

"You're taking it hard, man. You've had breakups before," Ben says. "What's so different about this one?"

"I thought Mary was the one. I always pictured myself marrying her, having kids, and living in our own house."

"Suburban life?" Jimmy asks. "Doesn't seem to suit you, Tony. You live in the middle of the city."

"I would give it all up if we could get back together."

"I'm flattered, but I have a girlfriend. She won't let me," Jimmy said, winking flirtatiously at Anthony. Again, everyone starts laughing. Annoyed, Anthony turns to Jimmy and says, "With Mary, not you, moron. I don't know why this breakup is weighing so heavily on me. I hear what you guys are saying, but I felt like she was my *special* one. I really wanted her to be that special one."

"Tony, your special one will come. In the meantime, enjoy your life and the company of your friends and family," Alec says.

"Easier said than done. How can I enjoy the company of you idiots?" Anthony says, realizing quickly that was the wrong thing to say, as his friends leaped forward and began slapping him on the head. "Ouch!" Anthony yells as he tries to dodge the hit.

"Serves you right," Ben says as the group calms down and resumes their banter until the waiter arrives with their food.

"Ah, food is here. Let's eat," Ben says.

Anthony is happy to be with his friends and having a good time. He knows it's a blessing to have close friends like these.

In the middle of their meal, Jimmy says: "Yo, don't you go to the ice rink every year?" "Not this year," Anthony replies.

"And why not?! There's a very nice lady in our office who has also recently had a breakup. I can set you two up. She likes ice skating, too."

"Not that your prior matchmaking efforts have been particularly successful."

"I'm not asking you to marry her. She's alone, you're alone. I can introduce you two losers, and you can spend some time together and go to the events you both like and not be losers anymore."

The other guys can hardly contain their laughter.

"Come on, Jimmy, don't punch the man below the belt," Alec says.

"I'm just saying. He doesn't need to take it seriously. No expectations, just friendly going out," Jimmy says.

"How do you know she likes to do the things I like to do?" Anthony asks.

"I asked."

"What? You actually asked her about the things I like?"

"Yes! I told her now that she's free, I have this loser friend who is also suffering from a breakup. Maybe you two can spend some time together. Then I told her what your interests are, especially around this time of the year. She enjoys those things too. Apparently, she's one of you Christmas fanatics."

"Jimmy, you went too far," Anthony says.

"Yeah, calling him a loser in front of a new girl," Alec interjects.

"Not that," Anthony says. "I know I'm a loser. I mean, asking her to go out before checking with me."

"Oh yeah. That too," Ben says.

"What's the harm?" Jimmy asks. "There are no expectations. It's just two people becoming friends and doing the things they have an interest in, together."

Anthony says nothing, but mulls the idea over in his mind. *It is a tempting idea. It wouldn't be a romantic date. Just going out for the holiday. But it feels like kind of cheating on Mary.* The thought seems ridiculous, since they've already separated, but in Anthony's mind, there is always a chance of getting back with Mary. *If that happens, then this will be cheating.* Turning to Jimmy, he says, "No. I'm not in the mood."

"Go ice skating and you'll get in the mood," Jimmy says.

"To the mood!" Ben exclaims as he raises his glass.

Automatically, they all raise their glasses. "To the mood!"

Jimmy, trying to mimic Aragon of the Lord of the Rings, adds, "What say you?"

"I'll get back to you on that," Anthony replies with a smile.

Happy Thanksgiving

One thing is clear. Anthony's mind has been occupied with his project and the Christmas party, and that is a good thing. He's gradually coming out of his shell. Over the past two weeks, he has managed to bring the project forward. This progress has made him happy, and he is beginning to enjoy work again. It's November 14, and next week is Thanksgiving. He is looking forward to spending the time with his family. As usual, Mom will cook the turkey and bake a pie. Most likely apple pie. His dad and two sisters love cherry pie, but they had it last year. It was only "fair" that they have apple pie this year. He could picture his sisters teasing him and calling him mama's boy for the pie, and him running after them. The thought brings a warm feeling to him. At first, he had doubts whether to face his family after the breakup. Deep down, he knew they would support him unconditionally, but he couldn't help feeling like a failure. However, these thoughts of family, apple pie, and the progress at work, give him the encouragement.

It's November 21, and he is packed and ready to go home to his parents. For Anthony, home is still where he grew up. Even though he's been living in New York for the past twelve years, it's Columbus, Ohio, that he considers home. The flight is in the afternoon. All morning he's busy with his project, wanting to wrap up his work before leaving town. There are some matters of the Christmas party that need to be finalized. He looks at his chat box and sees that Jasmine is online.

Anthony: *"Hey Jas. Do we have a list of venues for the party?"*

Jasmine: *"Hi Tony, I talked to the three that we agreed on. One of them is available."*

Anthony: *"How many ppl?"*

Jasmine: *"So far, with the clients, 200."*

Anthony: *"Hmmm ... too many?"*

Jasmine: *"The more the merrier. "*

Anthony: *"Do they have the capacity?"*

Jasmine: *"Yes, and they have their own planner who will take care of everything. We just need to choose what we want."*

Anthony: *"Awesome! The menu has to be confirmed with Lindsey. We need to know what will be suitable for the clients as well."*

Jasmine: *"Will talk to Lindsey. Aren't you supposed to be on your way to your parents?"*

Anthony: *"The flight is in the afternoon. I'm packed and ready. Just need to finalize work and this party thingy. Do we have a band? We decided to have live music."*

Jasmine: *"Yes. I have confirmation from the local band that you found. I watched their work on YouTube and they're ok."*

Anthony: *"Yes, I saw those videos, too. But we still need them to audition."*

Jasmine: *"I'll arrange with the venue and the band to have an audition after Thanksgiving."*

Anthony: *"Let's do it the day we come into the office. Killing two birds with one stone."*

Jasmine: "*Yeah, that'll be better. Have fun at home and, before I forget, Happy Thanksgiving!*"

Anthony: "*Happy Thanksgiving to you, too.*"

Waiting for Lindsey's response, he does some more work, then decides to leave a note for his colleagues wishing them a great time for Thanksgiving. He composes the email, finds a cute stock photo online, and sends it to the group. People start replying to that email and sending their own greetings. By the time he's done reading the replies, Lindsey pings him.

Lindsey: "*Jasmine told me about the menu and details of the party. What do you think?*"

Anthony: "*I think we should have a variety of food to accommodate people with dietary restrictions.*"

Lindsey: "*Agreed.*"

Anthony: "*It all depends on our budget. How much of it do we want to spend on the food?*"

Lindsey: "*I'm looking at their menu options and we should be good for the premium menu.*"

Anthony: "*Are we having VIP guests?*"

Lindsey: "*A few of our top clients, the VPs from our organization, and a couple of other VPs from other organizations. The CEO may join since we are inviting the clients.*"

Anthony: "*And you put this high up project in my hands? You want to see me get sacked?*"

Lindsey: "*LOL ... I want you to shine. This is a major opportunity for both you and Jasmine. For you, not only it'll take your mind off your troubles, but will help you get noticed.*"

Anthony: "*I thought my AI project would do that.*"

Lindsey: "*No PR is bad PR. Remember that.*"

Anthony: "*Then everything premium it is.*"

Lindsey: "*Yes.*"

Anthony: "*Okey dokey.*"

In the afternoon, Anthony wraps up his work, turns off his laptop, and walks around the apartment for an inspection to make sure everything was in place. He'll be out the whole weekend and doesn't want to leave any appliances on. Then he takes a 20-minute power nap. This is his way of boosting his energy before the flight. Every time he has a flight, he makes sure to have time for a 20-minute nap. In that way, he gets up energized and fresh, ready to tackle the unpredictability of modern flights – especially during holidays. Maybe it was the universe or the god of airliners, but whatever it was, his flight goes without any delays or mishaps. He arrives at his parents' late at night. The house looks the same except for the Thanksgiving decorations Mom and Dad had setup outside. Under the lights on the porch he can see there are three large pumpkins with one on a straw bale, on one side of the entrance door. Two pots of flowers one full of mums and the other sneezeweeds are placed on the other side. Mom has laid a few small white and orange pumpkins on the ground around the pots. Anthony stands there for a moment to admire the decorations. At the same time, he thinks what a source of comfort and sadness it is to see time has stood still in this corner of the world. He can't believe how an old and tired house can bring such comfort to his soul. It's as if all his troubles have gone away. This is the place where he grew up. The same place he did his homework and learned how to build a tree house from his dad. He is home.

His sisters are already there; Anna, the older one, along with her fiancé Walter; and Amber, his little sister. Walter works in a pharmaceutical company as a sales manager. Anna is a high school teacher. Amber is in her first year of residency to become a doctor; the first in the Russo family. Their parents are so proud of her. Anthony goes inside, where hugs and kisses are exchanged before the family sits around the fireplace in the living room for a quick chat.

"Tony you hungry? I knew your flight was late, so I left some food for you," his mother says.

"No Mom. I ate on the plane."

"How can you eat airline food?"

"Actually, it's not that bad."

"I remember when the food on flights was so good that people would lick their fingers. Flying was fun in those days," his father says.

"What are you talking about? Airline food has always been mediocre," Anthony replies.

"I don't know about that. All I know is, we would have much better food than what they serve nowadays," his father replies.

Anna joins the conversation, changing the subject. "Can we forget about food? We'll have a whole turkey in two days. Did you go ice skating?" she asks Anthony.

"Funny you mention it, Annie. We were talking about it with the guys some time back."

"That's not an answer. Did you go?"

"No, not yet. Maybe later in December, when the weather is a bit colder."

"Maybe I can come and visit you in December."

"Don't you have class?"

"No, Walter has some business in New York, and I want to go with him."

"I asked her to come with me. It'll be fun to see New York around the holidays," Walter says.

"How long are you planning on staying?"

"Walter needs to work December 11 and 12. We'll be there on Saturday to have time for some sightseeing."

"Why don't you two come and stay with me?"

"Oh no, we won't impose. But we'll plan on going out one night."

"I'll come and visit during the day when Walter is at work."

"Okay. Can't wait."

Anthony knows that this won't not be the first time Anna will be visiting New York during Christmas. She'd been there many times. This is their attempt to keep him company as much as they can. His family is trying to support him in a subtle way. Anthony sees through that, but he doesn't mind. In fact, he's happy to be loved by them. It's midnight now and tomorrow is the day before Thanksgiving, so Mom suggests everyone get to bed to be ready for the day. They have a lot to do to prepare.

It's the day before Thanksgiving. Preparations are in order. Everyone has their share of work. Mom and Dad have done all the shopping beforehand. While cleaning the house and cooking and prepping, lighthearted conversation and laughter fill the air. Everyone seems happy. Looking at them is enough for Anthony to feel better. He's among those who love and support him. They know about his breakup and are trying not to talk about it. This weekend is all about having a happy family time.

Some people have parents, some have friends who are like family, and some have siblings or relatives. We all rely on those who love us and support us, regardless of circumstances. We all need a source of comfort at times of hardship, and that source is our families; friends who stand by us, parents, siblings, spouses, and children. They're the ones who give us hope and encouragement for a better life.

It's Thanksgiving Day. They usually sit for dinner at four. The family wakes up early, has a nice breakfast together at seven, and then goes about their business. Mom is in the kitchen cooking, with the occasional help from others. Dad is watching TV and from time to time, goes to the kitchen to help Mom and steal a kiss. As he and his siblings grew older, they helped more in the kitchen, but the majority of planning and cooking was done by Mom. She still wanted to be in charge and serve the best Thanksgiving dinner she could. And yes, Mom reveals that she's making an apple pie, and as Anthony anticipated, Anna and Amber impishly call him mama's boy. After a day full of activities, fun, and talk, it's time for Thanksgiving dinner.

The family is gathered at the dinner table with Dad and Mom at each end. Anthony and Amber are seated on one side with Anthony close to Dad, and Anna and Walter are seated on the other side with Anna close to Dad. It's a typical family dinner seating, but with good china and a lot of hoo-ha! They say grace, the turkey is carved, and everyone gets their favorite piece, along with some side dishes. In the middle of dinner, Dad asks Anthony about his breakup with Mary.

"Luca dear, didn't we agree not to speak about Tony's breakup?" Mom says to Dad in a calm and demanding way.

"I am just curious. I liked Mary. I just wanted to know what the heck happened!?"

"Daaad! Maybe Tony doesn't want to talk about it," Anna says. Dad replies: "Okay!"

After a two-second pause, Dad turns to Anthony: "You want to talk about it, son?"

Amber bursts into laughter and everyone joins in. That is typical of Dad. Anthony doesn't mind. In fact, he wants to talk about it and get it off his chest. They can't pretend nothing has happened forever. He wants to tell them how disappointed he is.

"I don't know what happened, Dad. I thought she was the one. I wanted to ask her to marry me on Christmas Eve. Right here, in this house. But she said we weren't soulmates, and that has met hers. Some Gary fella!"

There was a brief silence in the room before Dad continues.

"Don't worry, son. These things happen. I was rejected by two other girls before marrying your mother."

"If only I knew," his mother says, "it would be *three* others."

Everyone laughs at Mom's comment except Dad. He's not amused.

"Then I would have found my soulmate. You tricked me." Dad replies jokingly.

Again, everyone laughs and the mood changes. That little talk helps Anthony to get things off his chest. He didn't know how to talk to his family about his breakup. But once again, Dad has come to the rescue with his bluntness. It was his well-known tactic for opening difficult discussions. Going straight to the point.

"Tony, all joking aside, these things are not all in our hands. We don't choose who we love, it just happens. It's okay to be sad about your breakup, but you need to move on. You never know what the future will bring."

"I know that, Mom, but it doesn't help. Everyone is telling me to move on. How can I? I feel like a loser. You and Dad had *me* at my age. I can't even keep one girl long enough to start a family. It comes so easy for many of my friends. Why is it so hard for me to meet the one?"

"It's not a contest Tony. You can't force these things. You just have to keep going. And also know that we are always here for you."

"Maybe that's it? Maybe every time I meet a girl, I don't put enough effort into the relationship because I know I can come back to you guys."

"Are you serious!? It's our fault that you can't find your soulmate?" Dad says.

"I didn't say that. I just think maybe I don't put enough effort into my love life because subconsciously, I know you'll be here to support me. I've turned into a momma's boy. At the first sign of hardship, I just run back to you guys."

"Do you really believe that, or are you trying to make an excuse?" his mother asks.

"I just want to know what's wrong with me?"

"There's nothing wrong with you, momma's boy!" Amber adds.

Everyone laughs and Mom says, "Amber, stop it. My dear Tony is not a momma's boy."

"Oooooh!" Anna and Amber exclaim simultaneously.

"Shut up," Anthony says as they burst into laughter.

Dinner is finished, and as usual, everyone loved Mom's cooking. After cleaning up the dishes, they sit in the living room for some coffee and apple pie. Anthony is glad he got everything off his chest, but he is still puzzled about his relationship with Mary and where it went wrong. He still loves Mary very much. It's as if he'll never get over it. But the room, the company, coffee, and apple pie make him relax and get this breakup off his mind for a while.

It's nighttime and Anthony goes to his bedroom feeling much better. The family got the details of his breakup, he had a good time for Thanksgiving, and his project was on track. He is relaxed for the first time in over three months. His mind is clearer now, and an idea starts growing in his head. A crazy one. Something he hadn't done for quite some time. It is childish, silly, and a bit embarrassing. At first, he laughs at himself for the thought. But the more he thinks about it, the keener he feels about it. What if he wrote a letter to Santa this year and asked for the most important thing he wanted? What if he asked Santa to bring Mary back, and they would be together? That's it. He makes up his mind. After all, what harm will it do to write a letter? He goes to sleep determined to write a letter to Santa on December 1 – just like he used to during his childhood.

It's December, let's meet strangers

The alarm goes off. It's five o'clock in the morning. December 1. The weather is seriously cold now with the prospect of snow. Snow during Christmas always makes Anthony happy. Yes, it's messy, slushy, and after settling for a few days, turns into ice and wreaks havoc on people. But for those who grow up in a snowy climate, a white Christmas is the source of great joy; and Anthony is no exception. He recalls how back home, every year around this time, if there was a snow, he and his sisters would go out and play. From making snowmen to snowball fights, they would spend hours outside running after each other. The outdoor Christmas decorations and white puffy snow on colorful ornaments and statues that looked like cotton would tempt them to stay out as long as possible. Then, when the cold would become intolerable, they'd run inside with rosy cheeks and sweaty foreheads, catching their breath and squeezing themselves in front of the fireplace.

Anthony stops the alarm, gets out of bed, and begins his morning routine. First, some morning exercise, consisting of calisthenics for twenty minutes. Then it's time for a shower, shave, and shampoo, after which he gets dressed. He usually has a smoothie or granola bar for breakfast. He tries to keep himself in shape. As usual, he turns on his laptop at seven-thirty and prepares his double espresso. As he sits down to work, he suddenly remembers the letter to Santa! First, he hesitates, but then decides to do it before getting cold feet. It's exciting and uneasy at the same time. He feels silly about it and smiles. He takes out a piece of paper and grabs a pen from his drawer, and starts writing the letter.

"Dear Santa,

This is Anthony Russo. I am thirty-two years old now. The last time I wrote to you, I was twelve. How twenty years have passed. I am a bit embarrassed to write this letter at this age. I hope you won't laugh at me. But if you remember, I always wrote to you asking for the most important thing I wanted.

Even though I have been a bit naughty, I have also been a lot good, and hope that you will see it in your heart to bring me what's in my heart. This year, Santa, I want you to bring me back Mary, my one and only love, so we will live together for the rest of our lives. Please make her see that I love her so much and will promise to make her happy all my life. This is the most important thing I want for Christmas.

Thank you and Merry Christmas.

Still feeling a bit silly, he folds the letter, puts it in an envelope and addresses it to "North Pole - Santa Claus." Then goes out and drops it in the mailbox. It's done. When he comes back to his apartment, he gets the feeling that he shouldn't have done that, but it's too late to have a second guess. Anyway, worst-case scenario, it'll get lost somewhere in the post office.

That night in bed, he is still thinking about the letter and what possessed him to do such a thing, when he gets another idea for the Christmas party. They could have a charity event to grant underprivileged children's wishes for Christmas through the letters they write for Santa. He thinks it'll be just like when he and his sisters got their presents that unfortunate year when their family didn't have enough money for gifts. They can team up with a local charity organization. He decides to discuss it with Lindsey in the morning.

The next morning, he lets Lindsey know of his idea. She puts it before upper management, and it's well received. They give him approval to find a trusted and reputable charity for the event. He asks Jasmine to help him find a proper charity and coordinate with them. Everyone likes the idea, and they ask how he came up with it, but he can't tell the truth. How can he tell them he wrote a letter to Santa, and that gave him the idea?!

It's December 12 and the morning is really cold. Anthony spent the day before with his sister Anna who is in New York for a few days with her fiancé, Walter. Since Walter was at work, Anna spent the day with Anthony and being the big sister, she decided to clean up his apartment. Against his resistance and explaining that a maid comes over once a week for cleaning and washing, she went on with the house work. Anthony was offering help but she insisted that he got on with his work and pretend she wasn't there. Two things were impossible, arguing with his big sister and ignoring her presence since every five minutes she would come to him either to ask for the location of stuff or complaining about his messy apartment. Anthony considers himself a metrosexual man. He tries to keep his apartment clean; his furniture and home décor are stylish. He enjoys the mid-century style. He's also very conscious about his appearance, his grooming, hygiene and clothes. Being an engineer, it seems out of character but he actually enjoys dressing up from time to time. So, it's annoying to hear her sister call him messy. However, Anna is a neat freak and cannot stand any kind of dirtiness. Her worst enemy is that speck of dust sitting on the table. It has to die.

This is the day of the week he goes to the office. But it's a bit hard to get ready for work since Anna reorganized almost everything to her satisfaction. Poor Anna just wanted to help her little brother out but Anthony was furious trying to find things from his socks which were in the wrong drawer to his keys and wallet. *She even misplaced my mind, I'm losing it Annie*, he thinks to himself while frantically going through every drawer to find everything he was looking for. He finally gets ready and rushes out. Usually on office days, he doesn't make his espresso. There's a cozy café at the corner of his street where he gets his double espresso and a croissant, so he heads there. As he is about to enter the place, a thundering voice from behind calls him.

"Anthony, is that you? Boy, you have grown up!"

Hesitantly, he turns his head around and sees a man in his fifties getting off of his Harley-Davidson cruiser. He is around six-foot-three, with a full salt and pepper beard and tattoos up to his neck. He's wearing jeans and a flannel shirt covered by a leather jacket. A typical biker. The man is looking at him and smiling. Anthony is confused. He can't remember knowing any bikers in his life. He is searching his memory to see if the guy matches any past teacher or distant uncle, or a neighbor, but nothing comes to his mind. As the man gets closer, it's obvious he's talking to him.

"Excuse me, do I know you?" Anthony asks.

"Well, yes, my boy. You know me very well."

The stranger directs Anthony inside the café and continues, "Brrrr, it's getting chilly in the mornings. I need a hot cocoa," he says as they enter the café.

They get inside and he still can't place that face anywhere familiar.

"I'm very sorry, but I don't recognize you. How do you know my name?" he asks.

With a wide grin, the man suggests they get their orders first, and then talk. When they both get their orders, the man directs him to an available table for a chat. Anthony politely asks him to make it brief since he's heading to work.

The man smiles and replies, "Well, of course. I'm surprised you don't recognize me." As he starts talking, he puts his hands on the table and Anthony can see letters tattooed on his knuckles. On the right hand, they read 'F.I.S.T' and on the left hand 'O.N.M.E.'

Fist on me!?

Now Anthony is a bit scared and curious as to what that even means! Does it mean you will have my fist in your face, or is it a pun for feast on me, meaning your face will feast on my fist, or perhaps he means lay a fist on me! Being a software engineer, he is swimming in these logical thoughts when the biker says, "Well?"

"Well, what?" Anthony asks.

"About the letter you sent me."

Anthony is thinking he never writes to anyone. It's outdated. He usually emails people, and with close friends and family, just texts them.

"I don't send letters. Is it something official?"

"Kinda! It is to me."

"Are you a government agent? Do you work for the IRS?"

"Why? Are you cheating on your taxes?" the biker says, winking and smiling.

Anthony pulls back, sits straight and says, "No! I never cheat on my taxes. I'm curious what letter you're referring to? As I said, I don't send letters. No one does these days."

"Yes, you did. You sent me a letter."

Anthony is more confused. This guy seems very sure about the letter. Then the guy puts his hand in his inside pocket, takes out a piece of paper and continues.

"This. You sent me this letter."

One look at the letter and he quickly recognizes it. It's his letter to Santa. How did this guy get hold of it?

"That's my letter. Give it to me," he quickly tells him.

The guy pulls his hand back and says, "No way. It's my letter. You sent it to me."

"I did no such thing."

"Yes, you did. You sent this to Santa." He then shows the top of the letter and says, "See? You wrote *Dear Santa*. It's mine."

Anthony is completely confused. He thinks this guy is probably deranged.

"What are you talking about?"

"That's what I was explaining. You weren't listening. I'm Santa! And this letter is from you."

For a moment, Anthony thought he heard it wrong.

"Did you say Santa?" he asks cautiously.

"Yes, my boy. I'm here because of this letter. I was surprised to receive a letter from you after all these years. Especially asking me for a girl. I usually deliver toys, and occasionally some bigger toys for adults. But delivering girls!" He nudges Anthony and laughs out loud.

"Will you keep it down? I never asked for a girl."

"Yes, you did. Here...," he says as he points to the part of the letter that reads *bring me back Mary*. He pulls the letter back and continues. "Mary is a girl, right? You asked for a girl."

A thousand thoughts go through Anthony's mind. He's thinking, for one thing, this guy couldn't possibly be Santa, because Santa isn't real. Secondly, Santa can't look like a redneck biker! Well, maybe Scandinavian. Immediately he comes to himself and thinks, *what are you thinking? Scandinavian! Snap out of it. He must have stolen the letter, or found it. Or maybe he works in the Post Office and is making fun of you.* He tries to compose himself, then turns to the guy and says, "Sir, you got it wrong. I didn't ask for a girl. I asked for you ... him ... whatever, to bring us back together. I don't know how you found that letter, but you can't possibly be Santa. Please give it back to me"

"Oh no, I'm afraid that's impossible. I keep all the children's letters."

"As you can see, I'm not a child, and that was a prank letter, so you can return it to me."

"My boy, in my eyes, everyone who writes to me is a child. I am so old that even a hundred-year-old great-grandfather is a child to me. Don't worry, Tony. I'm telling you the truth."

"Sir, please. Can you just forget about it? I'm late for work and really have to go now."

"Oh, I like your manners. You've been raised very well, my son. But I'm afraid I can't forget it. Once someone writes to me, I have to do my best to grant them their wish. Think of my reputation. What would people say if I failed to deliver? I am going to help you get your wish."

Anthony doesn't know what to say. He doesn't want to argue any further. He's mostly scared of "fist on me." He gets up and, as he walks away, just says, "I need to go. Keep the letter and forget about it; whatever joke you're pulling."

The plot thickens

The whole day at the office, all he can think of is his encounter with this strange man. What does he really want? Is it a blackmailing scheme, or some kind of scam to find where he lives and rob him? *What harm will it do?* he thinks to himself. He wishes he wouldn't have written that stupid letter. In this age of data, anything is possible, and nothing is private anymore. He curses himself all day long until it's time to head back home.

Tired, he drags himself into the elevator. He gets out onto his floor, and as he turns in the hallway, right in front of his door, stands the biker fellow. He can't believe it. Now he's beginning to get really scared. How did he know where he lives? Anger takes over. This guy was invading his privacy over a childish letter. It is time to confront him. Anthony is not a fighting man. He had never been in a real fight, never beaten anyone or cursed and yelled at people; even when driving. But he is determined to get to the bottom of this matter once and for all.

"Ah, you're finally home," the biker says. "Now we can get to your Christmas present." "How did you find my home? I'm mad now and going to call the police if you don't tell me what you want."

"But I told you. I want to help you get your wish for Christmas. Let's go inside and I will explain."

Hesitantly, Anthony turns the key, opens the door, and lets the man in. He directs him to the living room. The biker sits on the sofa, looks around to check out the décor. Anthony lives in a two-bedroom loft. The plaster walls are painted white and the one with the fireplace is all veneer brick. His mid-century sofa is the centerpiece of the whole design; it's bright brown fabric upholster with dark oak legs. The coffee table in front of it is also dark oak with glass top. He has a couple of transitional style armchairs with beige fabric upholster placed on each side of the sofa. He has a TV in front of the sofa. In another corner there's a turntable with a couple of speakers set on a console. His records are on a shelf under the record player. His dining area is large enough for his seven-piece dining set and a console on the side. On the walls he has a couple of large frames with prints of famous paintings. He also has a couple of monstera plants in large pots in the living and dining rooms. The biker says: "You've got a nice place here. I like how you decorated your home."

Anthony replies: "Thank you. Now spill! How did you get that letter? How did you find my home, and what is it you want?"

"Ok, I see you still don't believe me."

"How can I? You are not REAL!!!"

"But I am real and standing right in front of you."

"I mean Santa. Santa's not real. You're driving me crazy!"

"You remember when you were seven, and it took you two weeks to decide which toy it was that you really ... really ... really wanted?"

He even knows how I think, Anthony wonders as the man continues.

"And you finally made up your mind and asked for a Furby instead of that Star Wars action figure."

Anthony feels like he is going to pass out. *How in the world could he know that?* Anthony can't believe it. In a flash, he thinks, *maybe this guy is a friend of his dad's and knew about it. Or is he really Santa? Noooo, don't even go there.*

"Still not sure? How about when you were eleven? You finally went for that PlayStation Sega instead of Ninja Turtle figurines. On the one hand, you wanted to expand your figurine collections, on the other, that electronic game. Right? By the way, what happened to your doll collection?"

"They're not dolls, they're action figures! Still at my parents' house in a box in storage. But how do you know all this?"

"Because I'm Santa!"

"Even if I believe it, you can't be Santa. Santa isn't some big scary biker with tattoos!"

"How do you know? Have you ever seen me? Besides, don't you know judging people by their appearance is wrong? Shame on you. That's one point on the naughty list for you."

"I didn't mean to judge, but you have to admit, it's hard to believe. I mean, come on!"

"Deep inside, you know I'm right."

"Then why can't you just deliver my wish? What's all this fuss about?"

"It's complicated. You asked me to bring back Mary. I can't force people to move somewhere or fall in love with anyone. People are not toys or slaves, you know? I can't wiggle my nose and *poof,* Mary falls in love with you. Besides, do you really want that sort of love?"

"All I know is that I miss her and really want to be with her for the rest of my life."

"Then we have a problem, don't we? That's why I'm here. I need to know more about you two and see what can be done."

"And how do you suggest we do it?"

"Well, for starters, let's go grab a bite and a drink. You're tired and hungry, and I could murder a T-bone steak right now. Do you know a good bar with good food around here?" "I thought you travel the world to deliver toys. How come you don't know where to have a decent meal?" Anthony asks sarcastically.

"Wipe that smirk off your face. I don't do pit stops for food between deliveries. Mrs. Claus packs me some snacks and hot cocoa. But if you insist, I'll choose the place."

"Do I need to bring the car, or should we fly in your sleigh?"

With a damning look, the biker replies, "No need. We'll go on my bike."

Oh no, Anthony thinks, and says, "I'm not going to ride on that Harley."

"When did you turn into a sissy? It's fun. Don't worry, I am very careful."

Anthony is thinking, What kind of Santa talks like that? But it seems like an adventure, and he is peckish himself. Besides, it's something new to do, riding a bike with a stranger. *What could go wrong?* He immediately regrets that thought.

After a long ride in the chilly weather where icy wind hits his face constantly, they end up in a bar somewhere unfamiliar for Anthony. He is freezing, so he rushes inside. The first impression of the bar is that it wasn't too bad. It looks like one of those speakeasy bars from the Twenties; high ceiling, white table cloths, soft hue white light. The shelves behind bar are filled with bottles of drinks. There's a live band playing jazz music. Besides, the warm temperature inside is pleasing. The place is half full.

The bilker suggests they sit at the bar. Anthony also likes to sit at the counter. So far, so good. As they ease onto their tall barstools, the bartender comes over and asks what they would like to drink. Anthony goes for a pint of lager, and the biker orders a glass of milk. That order turns a few heads, including Anthony's. He looks at the guy with surprise and asks in a low voice, "Milk?"

"Yes. I like milk. It's good for you."

"We're in a bar, not a health club. We're supposed to eat fatty food and drink poison!"

"My body is my temple. That's what Mrs. Claus constantly reminds me."

"And I suppose you want to wash that T-bone steak of yours down with milk!"

"Listen; you do your thing your way, and I do my thing my way."

At this point, the witty and annoyed bartender asks the biker, "Pint, half-pint, or baby-bottle?"

"Very funny. In a glass, if you don't mind, Gary."

"You've been here before!?" the bartender asks.

"No, but I know you well."

Anthony looks at the bartender and recognizes the same curious expression on his face that he had when he met the guy. It's a source of comfort to know that he wasn't the only one being confused by this man.

Sitting next to them at the bar are three fairly large men, drinking pints of beer. Ever since the milk order, they were itching to make fun of the guy. While waiting for their drinks, the biker starts telling a Santa story about one of his present delivery mishaps. At this point, one of the three men turns around and introduces himself and his friends.

"Hi, I'm Bill. This is Larry, and that dude over there is Mikey."

"Nice meeting you. I'm Tony and this is ..." Anthony pauses to decide how to introduce this mysterious guy. He can't possibly introduce him as Santa. Then quickly he says, "Kris." He is thinking if this guy's Santa, then technically he hasn't lied!

"Chris, ... the milkman." His friends start laughing.

"So, what are you guys talking about? Maybe we can join in, if you don't mind."

Anthony is not the type to upset three well-built half-drunk men, so he replies, "We were talking about Christmas and Santa." The men laugh again.

"You mean that sicko who breaks into people's houses uninvited to take a peek at their children in their sleep?" The three guys laugh out loud. Anthony looks at Kris and notices that he's fuming. The situation becomes tense.

"Hey buddy, it's not nice to make fun of Santa,"

"Oh? And why not?"

Kris gets off his stool and slowly walks towards Bill, puts his hand firmly on his shoulder, and says, "Because I'm Santa, and I'm gonna put you on my naughty list."

Anthony is watching and realizes that "fist" is firmly gripping Bill's shoulder! He is both anxious and curious to see what the "fist" is going to do. With one foot on the ground, he's ready to leap forward and separate them in case of any fist fight.

Even though Bill is clearly annoyed by the hand gesture, the moment he hears Kris calling himself Santa, his eyes light up. He turns to his friends and, with a smirk, says, "You hear that? Milkman here thinks he's Santa!" The group of men starts laughing harder.

Kris calmly taps on his shoulder and says, "Bill, Bill, my drunk naughty boy. You just don't know what you're talking about. You see, I don't go to houses uninvited. People write to me and ask me to bring them presents. Have you ever seen anyone getting a present from Santa without writing first? You see? It's so simple that even that pea-brain Larry over there understands it." He turns to Larry and says, "Right?"

Larry is tipsy and confused and just says, "Right!"

Kris stares into Bill's eyes and continues. "See? And who told you I break in anywhere? Have you ever heard anyone complain Santa has broken into their home and they have to change locks?"

Bill doesn't really know what to say to this smart guy, so he just nods and mutters, "Yeah, right."

"Now all that aside, and most importantly," Kris continues. "I give children presents to bring some joy into their lives. Something you never comprehended. As usual, you haven't understood the meaning of giving. You should know that you've been on my naughty list for many years, you little mutt."

Anthony is wondering how this guy can be Santa. He's like a drop of water in hot oil–completely unpredictable. Right after Kris' remark, Mikey jumps into the conversation and says, "Ooooh, you upset Santa! Now he's going to put coal in your sock."

"Bill ... Bill ... I'm not gonna put coal in your sock, Bill. I'm gonna shove it up your ..."

Before he could finish his sentence, Anthony jumps out of his chair, pulls Kris back, and at the same time turns to the guys and says, "Why don't you guys have a round on us." Bill is already off his chair, ready to punch Kris, but with Anthony's offer of free beer, pulls back and sits on his chair. Kris also goes back to his chair as Anthony turns to the guys and calmly continues.

"Kris has been under a lot of strain lately. This is a busy time of year for him. Sometimes he thinks he's a real Santa. You have to forgive him."

Kris looks at him with anger and wants to correct him, but Anthony immediately turns to him and while staring in his eyes continues. "That's why he doesn't drink alcohol. Milk is good for his nerves."

They nod their heads in empathy and calm down a bit. Anthony signals the bartender, and he brings the guys another round of beers. The men seem happy with a round of free drinks. So, they all sit down and go back to their own conversations. The situation is defused and now Anthony turns to Kris and whispers.

"What kind of Santa are you, acting like that? Are you crazy? Do you want to get us into trouble? Look at their sizes."

"You forget I *am* Santa. I can handle three drunk morons." Anthony shakes his head and says, "Will you stop with that story? No one's falling for it. Besides, how can you be Santa, talking trash and fighting fight with people? Who are you and what do you want from me? Tell me the truth right now!"

"This again?!" Kris sighs. "Look, I've known these three idiots since their childhoods. They've been nothing but trouble. That's why Bill's wife left him and dear Mikey there is in the middle of a divorce. If I'm not Santa, then how do I know these things?"

"How should I know? You might have staged it. Are these your friends?"

"Don't be an idiot."

"Maybe you know these guys from before, or maybe you're just making things up."

"You think I'm making it up? Why don't you go and ask them?"

"Yeah right. You know very well I will do no such thing. This is part of your scam, isn't it?" Anthony pauses, then continues. "In any case, it doesn't matter how you know these things, whatever or however.

Just don't put me in the middle of a fight. I don't like to fight people. Especially big drunk people."

The bartender comes close, turns to Kris and says, "Are you ready to order or do you want to fight a bit more?"

Kris looks at him and says, "Don't you start with me, Gary. Or you'll go on my naughty list too."

Gary smiles and waits for the order. They eat and drink some more, then head back home. Kris drops him off at his building and rides his bike away. Anthony watches him disappear at the corner of the street, then heads back to his apartment, thinking about the excitement they had. It was a new experience for Anthony. In one day, he managed to meet a strange person, go out with him, and engage in an intense situation. The entire time, they did not speak about his relationship. Anthony is perplexed about the whole situation, but also hopes not to see this guy again.

I thought about Mary

The next morning, it is business as usual. Anthony rises and goes through his normal morning routine, fixes an espresso, and starts his workday. He is curious about this fake Kris. In one day, he managed to bring more excitement to his life than he'd had for the past four months. He wonders who Kris is, what's his real name, and where does he live?

Half an hour later, there is a knock on the door. It's Kris with a big bag.

"Good morning, my boy!" Kris says to Anthony with a wide grin. He seems to be in his cheerful mood. "Did you sleep well? We didn't get a chance to talk about your present."

"That's because you were busy fighting with some drunk men," he reminds Kris.

As Kris empties the contents of his bag on the dining table, he says: "You know, relationships are hard. You have to put yourself out there and don't be afraid to get hurt. It's like last night. You should not have been afraid to take a few punches from those guys."

"And end up in the hospital with a broken nose and ribs?" Anthony cuts him off. Now he's setting the table with what seems to be food containers and continues. "If you don't get hurt, how can you know your limits, your potential? Maybe you could overpower them, or maybe outwit them."

"I did," says Anthony. "That's how we dodged the beating."

"You bribed them to leave you alone. You were not ready to go in the water and get wet. That's my point. A relationship is like that. Do you know Mohammad Ali, the great boxer?"

"Yeah."

"He wasn't afraid to take a punch. He would go in the ring and endure the punches until he would find a chance to land his own. That's what made him great. He found his potential and challenged himself to get better. You see, love is like that. You have to get in the ring and be prepared to take punches."

He finishes sorting out the containers when Anthony asks what he has brought. To which he replies, "Breakfast! You should eat. That's a complete three-egg breakfast with bacon, sausage links, hash, pancakes, and coffee. We also have blueberry muffins and some fruit. I got myself an omelet."

"I never eat this heavy... well, only on holidays at home. Actually, Mom keeps feeding me stuff." Anthony says with a smile, picturing his mother. He can't wait to get home to his family. Only a few days left and then two weeks of complete relaxation and pampering. That's what holidays are for.

"Are you forgetting that we are in the Christmas timeframe? So, it's completely okay to indulge yourself."

They sit down. Anthony grabs the container, examines the contents, and then takes a bite. While eating, he turns to Kris and asks, "You also have a Christmas timeframe?"

"That's your thing, from the beginning of November, right?"

"Okay, how do you know that?"

"You still doubt me. Shame on you."

Anthony gives him a stare and has some more of the breakfast. It isn't bad, especially after last night's drinking. He had one too many. They continue with their breakfast until Kris is almost done with his food. He looks at his watch and says, "Goodness me, look at the time. I have to go to the North Pole for a quick check on the work. It gets very busy around this time of the year. But if you want, we can talk a bit more."

Not again with the Santa story, he thinks to himself. This guy must really take him for a fool. He also can't shake off the thought that he knows quite a bit about his life and thoughts. He turns to Kris and says, "Well, thank you for the breakfast and the cheap therapy session, but I have work to do."

"I can see that you're still not ready. We'll talk later." Then he gets up and leaves.

Curiosity gets the better of Anthony. He goes after him, opening the door and looking out to see which way he's going, but no one is out there. He is a bit puzzled. No one is that fast to get to the elevator or stairs so quickly. He doesn't put too much thought into it and turns his attention to work.

He closes the door and returns to his desk. As he sits down, he feels annoyed with this strange guy who showed up in his life quite suddenly and is messing with his love life. And all because of his letter that he probably found or stole.

That's it! he thinks. *Maybe he's a mail thief.* It's a ridiculous thought and he can't believe that anyone would break into a mailbox just to steal a letter to Santa. But at this point, he's willing to go with anything. On the other hand, he can't help but think about what Kris said. Maybe he had been cautious with Mary. Maybe he wasn't ready. Or maybe he's beginning to move on, the thought of which scares him. It means being stuck in repeating pattern of failed relationships and that's one thing he thought was over after Mary came into his life.

That afternoon, when his work is done, he gets up and starts pacing his apartment to stretch out. Then he realizes his apartment looks naked without the Christmas decorations. Suddenly, the place looks very awkward. For the first time, he didn't have a tree and other decorations. He misses them. Kris has certainly made him think deeply about his relationship. He goes to the kitchen to make a cup of cocoa. It's his favorite beverage during the holidays. His thoughts return to Mary as he stands in front of the living room window and stares at the street and the city. He has a great view from his loft, but hasn't enjoyed it much lately.

As he's watching people in the hustle and bustle of the holiday, he starts thinking about his relationship again. He loves Mary, that's for sure. But what if he hadn't shown it enough? What if he took her for granted? He's going through his memory, trying to find a moment or an occasion where he might have behaved in a way that would upset Mary. Maybe that day when he canceled on her because of an urgent meeting? Or the time she asked him to go shopping with her, but he refused because he was tired? Could these small things be the source of her breaking up with him? Then he remembers her words: "I care for you very much ... not soulmates ... Greg is my soulmate." What did she mean when she said she still cared for him? Did she still love him? Or was she just being tactful? He's giving himself a headache and doesn't want to think about it anymore. Maybe these little things were not the issue. That damn letter certainly is causing a lot of problems for him. How did this guy get hold of it?

It's six o'clock, and Anthony feels hungry. For the past three months, his eating has been irregular. He barely cooks. Not that his cooking is that great, but it's edible. His shopping has also become random. He goes into the kitchen, hoping to find some leftovers. He opens the refrigerator and nothing worth eating is inside. A thorough search of the cabinets doesn't help. All he's got are coffee beans for his beloved espressos. He needs groceries. He puts on his coat, grabs his wallet and keys, and goes grocery shopping. The grocery store is a block away, but outside, the icy wind is hitting his face and it feels like ages before he gets there. At the store, he starts with the produce section. He's looking and examining some tomatoes when a familiar voice calls him by his name. Surprise, surprise, it's Kris.

"What are you doing here?" Anthony asks.

"I'm shopping. What are you doing?"

"I'm here to watch a movie." Kris looks confused at Anthony's response.

"What do you think I'm doing here? Are you stalking me?" Anthony continues.

"Like I don't have better things to do. I'm here to get some food. Man's gotta eat."

"Okay then. Happy shopping. Bye-bye."

"Can't we shop together? We can talk while we shop."

"I knew it. You *are* stalking me!"

"I told you, for me to deliver your present, I need to know more about your relationship with Mary."

"I must be out of my mind. I don't even know why I want to discuss it with you. You're a complete stranger."

"Don't think of me as a stranger, but as someone who wants to help you. Is it wrong of me to try to help your relationship?"

"It's wrong in so many ways, but that ship has sailed. What do you want to know?"

"For example, did you two go grocery shopping together?"

"Of course, we did, all the time. Well, most of the time."

"Common food interests?"

"Almost. She likes fish and seafood. I'm not that keen on it. She likes sprouts in her salad. I can eat sprouts, but given the choice, I'd rather not. Why? Do we have to be compatible in food likings?"

"Not necessarily. But how did you plan your meals? Did you lean towards her taste more or yours?

"How should I know? I can't remember every minute of our lives. Maybe half and half. Are you done with your therapy session?"

"Oh, look at these orange juices. They're all pale. Orange juice should be ... duh... orange!"

"They're squeezed fresh daily. I don't buy the factory bottled ones."

"Oh, that explains it. They probably forgot to inject tranquilizers into these oranges before squeezing them. Poor things got scared and turned pale!"

"You *are* a comedian, but don't lose your day job," Anthony says sarcastically. "Speaking of which, what is your day job?"

"I'm Santa, I deliver presents. That's my job."

"Yeah," Anthony says, rolling his eyes. Kris is offended and they continue walking the aisle for more fresh produce. While walking, Kris goes back to their conversation. "I think you guys had more food that you liked than she. I know she didn't like meatloaf, but I bet you prepared it all the time."

"Actually, she would make a great meatloaf. Wait a minute, how do you know that?"

"Ah ... forget it. How about fish? Did you have a lot of fish for dinner?"

"Twice a week. But I never liked it."

"Did you ever mention it to her?"

"Yes, she knew. But since she liked it, I went with it. Is that wrong?"

"Not if you cooked it for her. She cooked meatloaf for you."

They keep talking and shopping. Anthony picks up a couple of cucumbers and lettuce for salad. At the same time, he is pondering on what Kris said, and remembers that he never cooked any seafood for Mary. In fact, every time they had seafood, he would make some joke about it. It never occurred to him that would hurt Mary's feelings. What if she wasn't happy about his show of dislike? Was that the reason for her leaving him? He is deep in thinking when Kris breaks his thoughts.

"Don't beat yourself up. She didn't leave you because of food."

Now Anthony is worried. Can this guy read minds? How did Kris know what he was thinking? He gives Kris a suspicious look. Kris looks the other way towards the onions and says, "You need these for cooking."

"You don't say!" Anthony says and reaches towards the pile and grabs a couple of yellow onions.

Kris picks up an onion and, while looking at it, says, "Did you know that Trolls have layers like onions?"

"Aw, you watched Shrek. How nice," Anthony says.

"I'm serious. Relationships are like onions, too. They have layers."

"Trolls have layers, relationships have layers. Relationships are Trolls!"

"Yours is trolling you," Kris said, giving Anthony a side-eye. Anthony is annoyed, but Kris's comment was actually very true. He turns to Kris and asks, "What's your point?"

"My point is, if you want to understand your relationship with Mary, then you need to peel these layers one by one and analyze them. For example, food. That's one aspect of a relationship. Did you ever think about your likes and dislikes, and how to agree on your meals?"

"You're joking. Do you think people spend time on their food likes or dislikes? It's food. You eat it. No questions asked."

"First of all, not everyone eats everything. People have different tastes. Secondly, it's important because it shows the level of your care towards the other person. People grow up with certain tastes in food and it becomes a habit. They hardly deviate from it. That's why everyone loves their mother's cooking, even if it's not so great. When you show care for the other person's taste, they will feel closer to you."

"I never disagreed with Mary over food. I just don't like certain things. But that didn't stop us from having them."

"Again, you also never cooked her favorite meals for her. Every time it was your turn to cook, you prepared something you liked. Did you ever prepare chicken dumpling soup for her? She loved it."

By now, Anthony was used to Kris' knowledge of this intimate information. He didn't know how he knew, but he also didn't want to waste time thinking about it. Sooner or later, he would find out. He also realizes that he had never cooked something solely to Mary's liking. That's a strange awakening. It never occurred to him to do so. So, he responds,

"You know what? For a biker, you sure like to get into the psyche of other people. Are you saying our relationship didn't work out because I didn't cook her favorite meals?"

"Don't think I didn't understand the sarcasm in that comment. However, smarty pants, just because I ride a Harley doesn't mean I don't understand human behavior. You're forgetting that I'm Santa and the human "psyche," as you put it, is the core of my business." He gives Anthony a smile and continues, "To answer your question, it depends on multiple layers. One layer is food. But she didn't leave you for food. She left you because she found her soulmate."

Anthony looks frustrated. He turns to Kris and angrily says, "About that. What exactly is a soulmate? How do you know someone is a soulmate? You know what I think? I think this is something made up by ancient folks just to tell amusing fibs. People always have differences. How can two people agree on everything? Even if that one-in-who-knows-billion happens, wouldn't it be a boring life? I don't get it."

"I'm with you on two people not being the same person. But soulmates are not the same people. Soulmates are people who fully understand and have great love for each other. That doesn't mean they think alike or share the same likes and dislikes."

Anthony got everything he needed from the produce section, and now they're in the canned food aisle. He grabs a couple of cans of baked beans. He also gets tomato paste and a can of peeled tomatoes. These are also good for cooking. At the same time, he gets back to their conversation and says, "But love is supposed to grow during a relationship."

"Yes, it is. Even between soulmates, love has room for growth. It's not like you reach the ninth level of consciousness and there's nothing beyond."

"Then how do you know if two people are soulmates?"

"By the amount of care and understanding they show in each layer of their relationship."

"I cared a lot about Mary and, I don't want to say fully, but mostly, understood her. I thought it was a work in progress and we would both improve on it with time. That's what I call a relationship."

"Don't forget breakfast. You're out of granola bars as well." says Kris.

Anthony's eyes open wide. "What? Have you been to my apartment? How do you ...?" He decides not to carry on that conversation and adds, "Forget it."

Kris looks at him innocently and says, "You know." And while pointing at himself continues, "Santa!"

They head towards the breakfast aisle and Anthony grabs his favorite bars. They continue shopping some meat and a couple of ready meals for those times he wouldn't cook. Shopping seems to be completed, so they head towards the cashier.

"Okay, I admit you gave me a lot to think about. But I still don't know how these talks can help get Mary back," Anthony says.

"If I know more about you two, maybe I can help you devise a plan to get Mary back by showing her how much you care."

"She knows I care about her. She knows she's my world. It's not me who has a problem, it's her. She left me, not the other way around. And she didn't leave for food; she left because she found someone else. Someone better. She used me."

Now Anthony is angry. If dealing with his breakup is like grieving, he has moved to the anger stage.

"She used you!? Do you listen to yourself? She plucked your flower and left you high and dry," Kris says sarcastically and laughs aloud. Even Anthony doesn't believe what he said, but he is angry and doesn't care. Maybe he is angry with Kris, or of coming to this deep realization about his relationship. The source of his anger is not important. He is just upset and wants to wallow in his own sorrow. They exit the store and Kris goes to his bike parked next to the store and says, "Sorry kid, I have to go and check on the work at the North Pole. We'll talk more later. Take care of yourself. And think about what I said."

Anthony was really upset now. Kris barges into his life, gives him some cheap advice and leaves. Not just leave, leave, like normal people. He goes to the North Pole! *Ew, what a game Kris is playing with me,* he thinks. The weather is cold, and the wind is blowing in his face. The way back home seems even longer. He gets home tired, cold, confused, and absolutely fuming. He has lost his appetite and decides to take a warm shower and go to bed. He takes an aspirin for the headache, which started after talking to Kris, stores his shopping in the pantry, and the refrigerator, and heads to the shower.

Let's get Merry and Bright

It's December 14 in the afternoon. Anthony just finished his work. This morning, Jasmine had some good news for him. She found a charity organization that was willing to team up with the company. The party is set for December 19 and they're planning on providing toys for twenty kids. The plan is to invite those kids to the party and hire a Santa to bring them their toys. It's going to be a fun event and an opportunity to remind guests of the virtues of giving, especially around the holidays when it's needed most. He's hoping that both sides–his managers and the charity–will agree to this theme. But that is a matter for their meeting tomorrow. Now he just wants to relax and enjoy this December afternoon.

At least that's what he thought. Very soon there's a knock on the door and it's Kris. *Oh no, not again*, he says to himself. Hesitantly, he opens the door and Kris walks in with his usual big smile.

"Hello my boy! I hope you're doing better today. How was work?"

"Tiring, but productive. Now, if you don't mind, I want to have a relaxing evening."

"No time. We are going out and we need your car."

"And where are we supposed to be going?"

"Getting a tree for this naked apartment. It's time you decorate this place," Kris says, then turns to Anthony. "Doesn't it look a bit awkward without Christmas decorations?"

Does he really read my mind? Anthony thinks. "I'm really not in the mood."

"Nonsense. You will get into the mood as soon as you start doing it. The first step is to get up and go buy that tree."

"Why does everybody tell me that?"

"Tell you what?"

"When I say I'm not in the mood, you lot tell me I'll get in the mood doing it."

"Then maybe you shouldn't say it!" Kris says, then adds, "Come on. Chop, chop. Move now, mood later."

"You're so pushy. Are you Santa or my mother?"

But he *had* thought of getting a tree and Kris, aside from being a nuisance, could be the sidekick he needs. So, he puts on his coat, picks up his car keys and off they go.

It's a cold evening and traffic is a nightmare. While waiting behind a red light, Anthony turns to Kris and asks, "Why did I listen to you? I was having a relaxing afternoon in my warm apartment. Every time you show up, I get into trouble."

"I'm not the one feeling awkward in that naked apartment. You are."

Anthony freaks out again. This cannot be just a coincidence. He looks at Kris doubtfully, wondering if he really is Santa. As a software engineer dealing with logic all the time, he knows it's impossible. He must be one of those great con artists.

"Let's get you in the Christmas mood," Kris says, and starts pushing buttons on the car radio, searching for Christmas songs. He finds one.

It's playing *Santa Claus is coming to town*, and he starts shaking himself to the tune in his seat. He turns to Anthony, winks, and says, "They don't know Santa is already in town!" and laughs hard.

"Will you knock it off? You can't convince me you're Santa. And the only reason I'm letting you in my life is to figure out your endgame."

"The endgame is my present to you," Kris replies with a wide grin. *At least he has the jolliness of Santa*, Anthony thinks. The light turns green, and they are finally moving when a car quickly cuts in front of them to cross the light. Immediately, Kris sticks his head out the window and yells, "Hey idiot! Watch where you're going."

"Get back in. Do you like to fight everywhere we go?"

"Didn't you see him cut right in front of you?"

"So? We'll take the next light. It's not like we're late for brain surgery."

"If this guy cut in front of my sleigh, I'd stick a coal up his ..." Before he can finish his sentence, Anthony jumps in and says, "Will you cut it out?" to which Kris replies angrily, "You don't stop cutting me off, I'll put a coal up your ..." Again, before Kris could finish his sentence, Anthony says, "That's it." He pulls to the side of the street, turns off the car and continues, "We're not going anywhere until you promise to behave."

"You're telling Santa to behave!? I'll put you on the naughty list."

"You should be on top of that list, going around swearing at people. And what's with you and the coal, anyway? Do you own a mine or something that you keep threatening to shove 'em?"

Kris is calm again and promises not to yell at the drivers anymore. They continue on their way.

They got to the tree lot where Anthony usually buys his trees. The lot has limited parking space, but they manage to find a spot. They spend about half an hour trying to find the right tree. Anthony doesn't like a couple of Kris' choices, and Kris finds some "aesthetic" flaws in

Anthony's trees. That's exactly how he described it. But they finally find a tree which both approve of. They buy the tree, bring it to the car, secure it on the top, and head back home. On the way back, the radio is still playing Christmas songs and carols, and Kris is dancing in his seat to every tune. Strangely, Anthony likes this side of him, and is enjoying his company. If he wouldn't fight with people and threaten to "coal them," he wouldn't be that bad of company.

Arriving home, they put the tree in the usual place. Anthony goes to his spare room and brings the decorations. They trim the tree and decorate every corner of the apartment. Christmas has come. After they're done, Anthony goes into the kitchen, makes a couple of hot cocoas, and finds a few chocolate cookies in the cookie jar. He puts them on a plate, puts the plate on the coffee table, and hands a cup of hot cocoa to Kris. Kris looks at the cup and says, "Where's the marshmallow?"

"Don't have any. Don't like them. Have some sugar."

Kris doesn't look very happy, but he goes on: "I see you got your Christmas cups out, too. Very nice."

"I gathered, now that we are doing it, let's go all the way."

"That's the attitude. You see, I told you your mood will change once you get the tree." Unfortunately, he's right. Anthony is feeling Christmassy. Then Kris asks, "Tell me, did you celebrate Christmas with Mary last year?"

"Before I went home, we did the shopping and decorations together. She couldn't come with me. I guess it was early in our relationship and she was a bit timid to meet my family. But she met the family on my birthday in April. And we went home together a couple of more times. Once for Mom and Dad's anniversary, then the Fourth of July."

"So, you didn't know how she felt about the holidays?"

"I think she was as excited as I was. Why?"

"No reason, just wanting to know more about you two."

"Look, I've let you in my life and told you a lot of things. Don't you want to tell me what's your real game?"

"Tony, my boy! You still doubt me. How many times do I have to tell you my intentions are only to give you what you really ... really ... really want for Christmas?"

"You ask me about Mary and give me some cheap advice. You go around and brawl with people and swear. I must admit, it's really difficult to believe you're Santa. Besides, how many times do I have to tell you, SANTA IS NOT REAL!"

"Ouch! You wound me," he says, pausing a few seconds before directing the conversation back to Anthony's relationship and asks, "How did your parents like her?"

"They liked her. Especially Dad. I think she liked them too."

"Are you sure? Did she tell you that?"

"She told me she liked them. Why? Was it not true?"

Anthony panics a little bit, as if Kris knew otherwise. Kris doesn't finish the conversation. He just puts the empty cup on the table and says he has to go. When he leaves, Anthony is left alone with more questions about his relationship. Why is it that every time Kris talks about them, he is left with more questions than answers? He is feeling more distant from Mary, as if he never knew her. Is Kris using reverse psychology on him? Is that why he puts doubts in his mind with those questions? Anthony has no answers. He looks around and smiles. At least he's beginning to enjoy the decorations.

Old friends to the rescue

The next morning it's work as usual. He and Jasmine get most of the party details organized. Everything seems to be on track. His project is shaping up and overall, it promises to be a good day. By evening, he's a bit tired, but pleased with the accomplishments of the day. Getting close to the holidays, it's important to have the work go as smoothly as possible. He wraps up his work and turns off his laptop. Tonight, he's determined not to answer any emails or check on messages. He wants to have a relaxing evening and enjoy his Christmas tree and the decorations. Maybe light music, some wine, and a classic Christmas movie.

Outside, it's raining and the monotonous sound of rain hitting the windows is so calming, Anthony decides to lie back on his chair and meditate for a while. Usually, when he is stressed or feels under pressure, he closes his eyes and tries to imagine himself in his happy place. He shuts his eyes and imagines being in the middle of a forest; somewhere like the Amazon rainforest. He imagines it's nighttime. He's in a tent, a small fire burning outside, making a crackling noise. Every now and then, a drop of rain meets the flare of the fire and instantly vaporizes in mid-air, creating a hissing sound.

As he is meditating, his phone vibrates. He had turned the sound off to enjoy the peace and quiet. There's a text message. It's from his friend, Johnathan. Anthony has been friends with Johnathan since primary school. They were two of a group of four kids who grew up together and remained friends. It's Anthony (Tony) Russo, Johnathan (John) Williams, Mark Gunners, and Hamilton (Ham) Knowles Jr. Hamilton hates his name. He thinks it's old-fashioned. Every now and then, he brings up the subject and says, "What was my father thinking? Why didn't my mom stop him?" To which the other three, usually in one voice, respond, "because she likes it!"

During these conversations, they suggest he have his name changed. In return, he says, "It's too late for me, but wait till I have my own son, I'll name him Hamilton III." At least that's what he used to say before his son, Daniel, was born. With two kids at home nowadays, he doesn't have much time to complain about his name. The friends did everything together, went everywhere together, and even spent nights in each other's homes from time to time. Their parents became close friends because of the kids. John and Ham got married, and Mark was engaged last year. He and his fiancé have planned to get married as soon as he returns from his trip to Europe. Mark works for an international financial company that operates global financial projects. Last year, they sent him to Bulgaria for one year to manage one of their projects. It was a great opportunity for him, and both he and Julia, his fiancé, were excited about it. It could mean a promotion and a higher salary. So, they sacrificed their time together for a better future. The guys still keep in touch, and every time Anthony goes home, they get together. Christmas is the best time for these friends to meet. Every year, they meet the day after Christmas. Usually, they pick a restaurant or a bar and spend the evening talking about their lives and events that happened throughout the year.

Looking at his phone, his first thought is that John is planning a get-together for this Christmas. He reads the message and finds out he's in town. He sends him a message and asks him to come over. About forty-five minutes later, John arrives. They hug and sit.

"What brings you here this close to Christmas?" Anthony asks.

"I'm here on an urgent matter."

Anthony looks at him and is worried something unfortunate has happened.

"What's happened? Everything okay?"

"No, it's not okay. Two months ago, Bibi saw a necklace in the window of Mr. Simpson's Jewelry. She liked it very much." His wife's name is Briana, and everyone calls her Bibi. "Right then, I knew what I was gonna give her for Christmas. Last week I went there, and it was gone. I couldn't find another one like it anywhere. So, I decided to come to New York and try my luck. Man, this city of yours sucks! What's with all this crime?"

"I haven't seen much crime. It's pretty safe around here. Forget the crime. How are you going to find it? How many stores have you visited?"

"I've been trying most of the known places. I've walked so much that my shoes got holes in 'em."

Yes, he looked pretty beat. Anthony says, "You scared me. I thought something serious had happened. No worries, tomorrow we'll search together."

John gives him a smile and says, "I FOUND IT!!" He starts laughing while taking the box out of his pocket.

"You bastard!" Anthony responds and joins in the laughter.

"Christmas is saved! I really didn't have anything to give her. She would kill me. I think she knew I was getting her this necklace."

"Dude, your marriage is saved. I was going to prepare the guest room for you." They both continue laughing until Anthony pauses to ask John if he had eaten yet.

"No, I'm starving," his friend replies.

"Go see what you can find in the fridge. Bring me some too."

"Ahoy, I'm the guest. You're supposed to serve me, not the other way around." While he's going to the kitchen to see what he can make for their dinner, he continues, "Can't you see I'm tired?"

John is a chef and works in a restaurant. Since childhood, he had a taste for food and his friends learned to trust his judgment in that area. He is the one always recommending restaurants and bars. So, it was a treat for Anthony to have him there. He was anxiously waiting for his gourmet dinner.

"I will lie down on this sofa on your behalf, so you'll be rested."

"Shut up and come here and help me. If I'm cooking, you're going to be my commis chef."

"What's a comic chef?" Anthony asks, intentionally mispronouncing the word.

"You're the comic chef. The idiot who doesn't know how to cook," John answers as he throws a potato at him and says, "Peel this." He puts another potato on the counter and says, "And this one."

"Two potatoes! Our lucky night. Chef's preparing potatoes for dinner. One each!" John does not respond, but glares at him.

John prepares a quick stew with chicken, curry, and some vegetables. They set the kitchen table and sit for dinner. Anthony smells the food and says, "Smells good. I can't believe you did this in half an hour."

"You can do it yourself. You know, I'm surprised. You have all this fresh produce in your fridge, and you have meat in the freezer, but don't cook. Why do you even bother with shopping?"

"I cook. But lately I haven't been myself," he pauses before continuing and changing the subject. "This is your busiest time of year. You could buy that necklace online or just buy it and head back home. What exactly is going on?"

"I wanted to see you and know what's going on with you? You came for Thanksgiving, but we didn't catch up. You just sent a text, and that's it. We're worried about you."

"Does Bibi know you came to see me?"

"I skipped the necklace part, but yes, she knows. There's a restaurant owner here who is interested in buying our business. I came to have a talk with him."

"You want to sell the restaurant? Why? What are you going to do?"

"It's not like that. Actually, it's a great offer. He wants the restaurant, but not the name. We keep everything, but change our name to theirs. Kind of like a franchise, only in gourmet dining. He was at our restaurant about two months ago and I think he liked it. I got a call, and we had some talks, but he wanted me to see his restaurant and go through the details. Bibi and I are both excited. We get his support, and he will benefit from his franchise. But don't change the subject. What's going on with you?"

"You know what's going on. This breakup was hard on me."

"You've had breakups before. Quite a few of them, I thought by now you'd be used to it," John said and smiled.

"Everyone keeps saying that. Why don't you people want to understand? This one was different. She was the one."

"If she's really the one, then why the heck aren't you trying to get her back? But I don't think that's the real issue. It's me, remember? We grew up together. I know you better than my brother. What is really bothering you?"

"I guess the truth is, I feel like a failure. I think I'll never measure up to my family's expectations, especially my dad's."

"Mr. R's expectations? What expectations? As long as I've known him, he has never forced you to do anything. He's always been supportive and understanding. What are you talking about?"

"I know he and Mom don't force me into anything, but I can feel it. Look at my dad. I was actually telling them about the breakup at Thanksgiving. He ran a family, raised three kids, bought a house, and made a future for all of us. Then there's you and Ham. You guys have kids already. Even Mark is engaged. I'm 32! And what am I doing? Sitting here drinking coffee."

"Are you seriously competing with your dad and us? Have you completely lost your mind? Since when has marriage turned into a competition? First of all, they were a different generation. Today's culture and environment are different."

"Pfff! We're not talking about the 40s or 50s. They married in the 80s. It's not like they were completely different. Eggs weren't two cents a dozen. Okay?"

"Nevertheless, the culture was different. This generation is less inclined towards a formal marriage."

"Yeah, that's why three of my childhood friends are married or engaged!"

"And that's the second thing. Everyone's different. We found what we were looking for. It's not like we reached a certain age and decided to marry. For you and many others like you, circumstances are different. You haven't found the right woman yet. Maybe you'll find your true love one day, or maybe not. This is not something you can force. It's not a checkbox on your bucket list to tick."

"Pah, you talk just like Kris."

"Who's Kris?"

Anthony realizes John doesn't know about Kris, and he's not prepared to tell him about the whole ordeal. At least not yet. Maybe someday in the future, he'll tell the story as a funny anecdote, but not today. Instead, he says, "This biker guy who follows me everywhere. He keeps telling me the same things you just said."

"Hold on. Back off. What biker guy?

"There's this guy with tattoos and a bike who keeps pestering me. He pisses me off. Comes to my apartment, meets me outside; he's everywhere. And he keeps giving me cheap advice like this."

"You have a biker who's stalking you?!! You *really* have lost your mind! This city is getting to you, isn't it? Have you called the police?" John asks, the worry showing in his voice.

"It's nothing. He seems harmless. And no there's no need to call the cops. Actually, he helped me with the Christmas tree and decorations."

"I can't believe what I'm hearing. Is he your friend?"

"God, no! Last thing I want is him being my friend." Anthony pauses for a moment and continues, "I don't want to see him again. But I'm pretty sure he'll show up any day."

John is completely puzzled by Anthony's erratic response and asks, "Who is he? Are you sure he's a biker? Is he in a gang or something? Where does he live?"

"No, he's not in a gang. He just rides a Harley. I don't know where he lives. Probably the North Pole. At least that's what he tells me."

"I'm worried about you, man. What do you mean, the North Pole? You're not on drugs. Are you?"

"No! That's what he says. Anyway, it doesn't matter who he is or where he lives. He can live on the moon and fly to Earth like Mighty Mouse as far as I'm concerned. You all think that one day I will find my true love. Well, news flash: I already did. Mary is my true love. And I lost her. That's what bothers me. That's why I feel like I've failed."

"I don't know about this Kris guy and how you can be so casual about a stalker. How you even discuss your personal life with a stranger, eludes me. I think for your own sake, and for the sake of your sanity, you need to see a psychiatrist. Talk to a professional. Whatever you do, you need to snap out of this. You're getting to the edge of depression."

"I'm not depressed, and I will not go to a shrink. If they knew anything about the human psyche, they would sort out their own lives, wouldn't they? Every one of them has their problems. How can a troubled person give me advice on not being troubled?"

"You always had this misconception about psychiatrists. These doctors are professionals. They won't let their personal lives interfere with their work. It's like saying doctors should not get sick, or chefs should have gourmet meals at their homes every day."

"So what you're saying is, they don't know what they're talking about. Why should I rely on something so irrational?"

"You're irrational. They don't know everything, but whatever they know helps people to figure out some of their issues. It's either that or talking to biker stalkers from the North Pole! You figure it out."

"Very funny. Good thing your cooking is better than your insults." Anthony says. "I'll be fine. I just need to sort some things out on my own. We have two weeks of holiday. When I get home, we'll definitely get together."

"Just take care of yourself and know that you're not alone. You have all of us. We won't rest until get you married to the right girl." They both laugh.

At this point, they are finished with their meal and have cleaned up the dishes. They retire to the living room to watch one of their favorite

Christmas movies they used to watch as teenagers, Die Hard, what else? Yippee ki-yay! Anthony is grateful to have good old friends. They're a source of comfort. In the morning, John calls for an Uber to take him to the airport. Anthony is feeling much better knowing that his childhood friend took the trouble to come and visit him. Even the distance and busy life cannot sever their friendship. He promises to keep their tradition of meeting the day after Christmas. Apparently, Mark will be coming home, too. The gang will be together for a few days. John leaves and Anthony goes to his desk to start his workday.

Don't panic, Santa Claus is in town

Anthony hasn't seen Kris since the tree-trimming evening. It's been four days now. He's getting worried. Not that he misses him—well, maybe a little bit. He's mostly worried about his shenanigans. He might be planning something. At least when Kris was around, he could watch him closely. He is working on his project when a ding from his messenger grabs his attention. It's Jasmine.

Jasmine: "We have a problem!"

Anthony: "Oh, no! What now?"

Jasmine: "The Santa we hired for tomorrow is a no-show. He called in sick."

Anthony: "Can you blame him in this weather? Let's find another one."

Jasmine: "From where? All Santas are busy. 'Tis the season."

Anthony: "What are we going to do?"

Jasmine: "You're asking me? I'm asking you. You're in charge. lol …"

Anthony: "Let's get Lindsey."

"Jasmine: "Ok. Better to have a meeting. I'll send the invite."

Two minutes later, the invite arrives for a quick sync-up. Anthony turns on his camera and joins the meeting. Lindsey and Jasmine are waiting for him. They all look at each other and laugh at their misfortune. Lindsey begins the conversation. "Guys, we have a problem. If we don't get a Santa, the whole theme will be ruined. It'll be quite embarrassing. Has anyone reached out to the charity to see if they have anyone?"

"I already talked to them," Jasmine said. "They don't. But I have an idea. How about we make Tony Santa?" They all laugh.

Suddenly, in the background of Anthony's screen, Kris appears.

"Hello! Am I interrupting anything?" Kris asks.

Anthony is so shocked he almost jumps out of his chair. He turns to Kris to ask what he is doing there and how did he get in. Before he can even say a word, Kris leans over Anthony, towards the camera, and waves to Jasmine and Lindsey.

"Hello there. I hope I'm not interrupting anything," he says. Turning to Anthony, he whispers: "Did I startle you?"

Anthony turns to the camera and says, "This is Kris, umm ... my neighbor. Give me a few seconds. I'll be right back. This may be an emergency." He quickly turns off his camera and mutes his mic, then turns to Kris and angrily demands to know how he came in.

"Did you make a copy of my keys? How did you get in and what are you doing here? Don't you see I'm in the middle of a meeting with my boss?"

"I don't need a key. I used my secret passage," Kris says, winking slyly at him.

"This isn't funny. We'll talk later. Now shoo. I have a meeting." Anthony quickly returns to his meeting, apologizing to Lindsey and Jasmine.

"It's ok. What do we do with the Santa problem?"

Before anyone can say anything, Kris jumps in front of the camera and asks: "Did you say Santa problem? No worries, I'm here," he says, and smiles his usual wide, jolly grin.

"No, that's ok. If you don't mind, we have a meeting." Says Anthony.

"Lindsey said you have a Santa problem. I'm Santa, and I believe I can help."

"You know my name!" Lindsey exclaims.

Anthony thought, *oh ... oh, if this guy opens his mouth and starts talking nonsense, I won't be able to go to work anymore. I'll have to quit. Maybe even relocate to another city.* So, in a flash, he says, "Your name is under your picture."

"Oh yes. Well Kris, is it Kris?" Kris nods. "You said you're Santa."

"Aha."

"Are you working at the moment?" she asks.

"Well, this is my busy time of the year. But not too busy for helping little kids get their presents at your party."

"Oh, Anthony has told you about our party! That's great. But are you sure you can be Santa? No offense, but you have a lot of tattoos, and I don't think children would believe it."

Anthony is looking down and shaking his head. He can't believe the situation. Four days Kris was missing, and now he has to show up in the middle of his meeting. Worst of all, Lindsey was about to employ him. This was a disaster. But when Lindsey mentioned the tattoos, it was like a light at the end of the tunnel. A lifeline for Anthony. Immediately, he agrees with Lindsey.

"Yes, I don't think it'll work, Kris. I know you want to help, but we will manage," he says, then jokingly adds, "As Jasmine suggested, maybe I will be Santa!"

"What's with you people and my tattoos?" Kris says. "Don't worry, I will be wearing that big beard, so my face and neck are covered. I'm also wearing white gloves, which are part of the costume. Everything will be covered. Kids won't notice a thing."

"Hey you're right. This might work. I didn't mean to offend you, Kris. You're Anthony's friend, and that's a good enough reference for us," Lindsey says.

Anthony wants to correct her, but Kris pokes him on the side while staring at the camera.

"Can you give us a quick demonstration of how you're going to be Santa?" Lindsey asks.

"No problem." He pauses for a moment, then straightens himself, clears his throat, opens his arms, and while looking in the abyss as if talking to the kids, with a loud and deep voice says, "Ho ... Ho ... Ho ... Merry Christmas!" nodding his head at the same time. He pauses for a second and then looks at the camera and asks, "How was it?"

"Very good." Lindsey and Jasmine reply, both clapping.

"I think you can pull it off," Lindsey says.

"Yes, that was good. I believed it," Jasmine agrees.

Oh no, Anthony is thinking to himself. *If this guy goes to that party and someone says something or makes fun of Santa, he'll start a fight and it'll be disastrous.* He wants to cry right there in front of his boss, and he doesn't even care. Contrary to how he is feeling, Kris looks very pleased with himself.

"There's a matter of your compensation..." Lindsey begins. Before she finishes her sentence, Kris says, "No charge, I'll do it for free. I have my costume and all the Santa gear!"

With his head down, Anthony whispers, "Yeah, bring Rudolf, too."

Kris pokes him again without taking his eyes off the camera.

"This is very generous, but it's your work. Are you sure?" Lindsey asks.

"Consider it my donation to your good cause," Kris says.

"Tony, you never said you have such a wonderful friend. Kris, I'm very happy to meet you," Jasmine says.

Anthony, putting on a smile, says sarcastically, "Yes, Kris is such a wonderful friend. Wonderful ... wonderful friend." Kris gives him another poke on the side.

"Thank you, Jasmine. Maybe this afternoon we can get together and you can see me in full costume," Kris says.

"That'll be nice, but unfortunately, I have work to do at home. But tomorrow, Tony and I will be in the venue for final arrangements. If you come in early, we can do some rehearsals."

"That's great! I'll be there."

"Phew, Kris to the rescue! Tony, your friend saved our party," Lindsey says.

They end the meeting and Anthony looks at Kris angrily and says, "This is unbelievable. You go away for four days. I don't know what you're cooking up for me. Then you barge in without invite and disrupt my work. What I want to know is, how did you get in?"

"If I'm not mistaken, I just saved *your* behind in front of your boss. Weren't you guys desperately looking for a Santa?"

Anthony acknowledges Kris is right on that part.

Kris continues: "You wanted to be Santa? What a laugh. The kids would be so disappointed."

"What are you talking about? I can be Santa."

"Yeah? Do a ho, ho, ho."

Anthony, trying to act like a Santa, mumbles quickly, "Ho, ho, ho!"

"Heh, heh, heh. You botched it, my boy. Leave the matter to the professionals."

"Don't change the subject. How did you get in?"

"The way Santa always gets in when bringing the presents."

"If you have any copies of my keys, I want them back please," Anthony says, putting out his hand.

"I promise you, no keys. You can search me. And if you don't find keys, I'll punch you in the nose."

Anthony thinks Kris is playing with him. Maybe he had forgotten to lock the door. He calms down a bit, and it hits him that Kris showed up exactly when they needed help. Another coincidence? Or something else?

"What brings you here, anyway? I thought you were out of my life," Anthony asks.

"I still have a problem with your present. How can I go away? I promised to give you your present, and that's what I'm going to do."

"Do you always go to these lengths for all your customers?"

"Where do you think I've been? I will do my best to deliver exactly what people need."

"Who's the other victim? I mean customer!"

"Santa victim confidentiality!" Kris responds with a straight face.

"Okay, but you still haven't told me why you're here."

"Oh, I almost forgot. There's a new place I found with the best Italian food. I came here to tell you not to plan anything for dinner tonight. We're going there."

"You couldn't wait till this afternoon?"

"Santa for the party, remember?"

"How did you know we were looking for a Santa?"

"What's the point of telling you? You wouldn't believe me, anyway." After a short pause, he continues. "Okay, Will, the Santa that you guys hired, is a friend. I didn't see him in his usual spot, so I went to his place to see how he was doing. He has a bad cold. We barely talked, but he told me that there was this event he had to cancel. After explaining the whole thing, I connected the dots and figured out it was your company's party. Naturally, I knew you wouldn't be able to find another Santa in such a short time. I came here to tell you I'll do it. You were already in the meeting. So, that's that."

Anthony has a mixed sense of relief and surprise. He is relieved that the whole thing was so logical, and no tricks were involved. He was also surprised that Kris actually explained it to him. He could have led him on in believing it was an act of magic.

"Fine, let's try this new place. I've got a lot of work to do now." Anthony says.

"And I have to go back to the North Pole. I'll see you tonight," Kris said as he left the apartment.

Anthony is frustrated with these Santa performances of Kris, but he has to know what Kris' intentions are. Besides, Italian food sounds good.

Get real, fast

That evening, Kris comes over. He is wearing an evening jacket and looks sharp. He suggests Anthony put on a jacket as well, and the two of them head out to the place Kris recommended. The atmosphere is posh. It's a high-end restaurant, and Anthony is surprised that Kris recommended this place.

At first glance, Anthony thinks this is the kind of place he would bring Mary for a nice romantic dinner. He is suspicious of why Kris has chosen this particular restaurant. It's a bit uptight for his taste. Kris comes inside behind him, and they wait for the hostess. As she turns her attention to them, Kris says, "Reservation for Klaus."

Anthony is more surprised that Kris made arrangements beforehand. *Klaus! He never quits*, Anthony thinks. So far, everything he is doing this evening seems out of character. They are seated and the waiter hands them the menus and leaves the table. Anthony turns to Kris and says, "Nice place. How did you hear about it?"

"Someone wrote about this place in their letter to me. I thought we might give it a try."

Anthony just smiles. At this point, he is beyond arguing about Kris' identity as Santa. He just considers it his quirk and moves on. "It seems a bit out of your character."

"Why? Because I ride a bike? Or have tattoos?" he says. Then he adds, "You think I shouldn't enjoy the finer things in life?"

"I didn't mean it that way. It's just that ever since the day I saw you, you had nothing on but jeans, leather jackets, or a flannel shirt. You're quick to get into fights. You're rude, intrusive, and quite a pain in the butt. It's hard to believe you would enjoy a place like this," he says, smiling.

"Thank you for all the nice things you said about me. For your information, I do enjoy *these* kinds of places. Besides, sometimes it's good to confront your daemons. It builds up character and helps you learn something about yourself."

"And we're back to cliché?!"

"I wouldn't dismiss cliché so easily. There's a reason some things are cliché," Kris says, holding his fingers in the air, making air quotes. "You may laugh at them, but they have proven their validity through the test of time." Looking at the menu, he continues, "Shall we order?"

Anthony is completely baffled by Kris' behavior. It's as if he is a different man.

They order their drinks and food. Anthony turns his head to have a quick look at the place. It's a warm atmosphere. There are a few paintings hanging on the walls. They seem to be copies of famous paintings. The walls are off-white, and the chairs are oak stain. It's obvious that the owner has tried to adopt a transitional style with a mixture of modern and traditional. He thinks the design works. And that the place is packed is a testimony to that. A restaurant like this is expected to be busy at this time of the year. He adjusts himself on his chair to get more comfortable.

At this moment, Kris is staring at a table behind him. He looks at him curiously. Kris notices Anthony's questioning gaze and asks, "Isn't that your ex, Mary?"

His heart starts beating in his mouth as he quickly asks, "Where?"

Kris points in the direction behind him. "There, the third table."

Anthony panics, "Put your hand down. Are you sure?"

"Of course, I'm sure. I've known her since her childhood!" Kris says, then continues with a louder voice. "It's Mary! Turn around and look for yourself."

"Shush! Keep your voice down. I don't want to look." Anthony keeps talking. "What is she doing here?" He is filled with mixed emotions. He is happy to see her again, and at the same time, is anxious about how she will react if she sees him. He asks Kris, "Is she with someone?"

"Yes, I think it's Gary. I know him too. Just like you, on my nice list."

Anthony is irked by the thought. He wonders if that is because of jealousy. *What else can it be?* he thinks. He knows he's jealous of Gary. So much so that without having seen him even once, he wants to punch the guy in the face. It occurs to him he is in the middle of yet another coincidence. He angrily says, "You knew she would be here. That's why you brought me. How did you know?"

"Humble moi?! What makes you think I know of these things? It's not like I'm Santa and know stuff," Kris responds.

Anthony is boiling inside with anger. He doesn't know whether or not to believe him. But right now, all of that is irrelevant. He says, "Oh, shut up! You keep messing with my life. I wish I had never sent that stupid letter."

"If you don't want to see her or talk to her, then don't. Pretend two strangers have come to the same place for dinner. It's not like I'm pushing you to her table," Kris says, continuing to stare in her direction and now smiling at her.

Anthony slides a bit lower in the chair and says, "What are you doing? Now you're smiling at her? Are you mad?"

"Relax, she hasn't seen you. Our eyes met, and I was just being polite."

"Stop it. You're never polite. Don't start now."

Kris glares at him. "You're acting like an impertinent child. You're this close to going on my naughty list," he says, showing a pinch gesture with his fingers.

Anthony's eyes widen and he looks directly at Kris. "That's it!" he says. "Put me on your naughty list. Don't bring me my present. Goodbye. Let's get out of here."

"What's with you, boy? You're having a heart attack. Take it easy. Just sit there and enjoy your evening. Pretend she's not there."

"Then stop looking at her!"

"She's in my line of sight. I can't keep my head down all the time. She'll get suspicious."

Now he is just messing with Anthony. Their drinks arrive, and Anthony grabs the glass and gulps down the contents. He wipes his lips and before the waiter goes away, orders another one.

He wants to turn around and look at her. He misses her. But he doesn't find the courage. He's embarrassed to be called ex in front of the new guy. Time has stopped for him and it's not moving forward. This agony seems endless. A few minutes ago, he was beginning to relax and enjoy the atmosphere. Now it has become unbearable. Why did Kris bring him here? Does he have a plan to bring them together, or is he just playing a game? He doesn't understand any of this. A few minutes later, the food arrives. He seems to have lost his appetite. Kris has been quiet. Anthony is just playing with his food.

Kris opens the conversation: "If you are really in love with her, then go and talk. This is your chance."

"And what would you have me to say? Hey, I'm stalking you. Please come back."

"Don't be cynical. You are here by chance and just noticed her. It's polite to go and say hello. It'll give you a chance to assess your situation."

"What if she doesn't like it? What if she gets mad?"

"You know her well, or at least should know her after all this time. Do you think she's the type of girl to get mad if you go and say hi?"

"No. I don't think so."

"Maybe you value your pride more than her love?"

"That's not true. I love her very much."

"Are you in love with her enough to swallow your pride and go over there? Is seeing her worth that much, or are we playing it safe again?"

"What's your point?"

"The point, my son, is that you have to make a decision about which is more important to you. Mary? Or the thought of Mary?"

"I don't understand."

"If you are in love, then you go in that ring and take your punch and be happy that you see her one more time. You're going to face your daemon. You grab this opportunity and try to present yourself. You seize the moment." Kris pauses for a second and continues, "Or you just want to love Mary because you think this is your last chance for happiness. You love to think of Mary and what could be."

"Do you doubt my love for her? I'll do anything for her."

"I have no doubt that you want to love her. But in all those lovey-dovey snapshots of a happy life that you picture in your mind, have you ever once thought of real life? A mortgage, children's tuitions, fights, disagreements?" He continues, "Have you ever considered what would real life be like with her in, say, five years, or ten? You were with her for a little over a year and life was sweet. Very few disagreements and even fewer quarrels. But you want to spend the rest of your life with this woman, and you can't even go there and say hi to her because of your pride. Ask yourself one question: Are you in love with her enough to get up, go to her, and say hello?"

Anthony is beginning to understand. It's as if the clouds are clearing in his thoughts. Suddenly, he didn't miss her as much as he thought he did. Could Kris be right? Was it the thought of Mary that kept him going? He wanted to get married and find happiness, and Mary was the closest thing to that happiness. Was it a misconception? He is trying to understand if he is truly in love with her or just wants to do what he thinks is the right thing to do?

He has watched his parents' life together, and his friends who are married, and has concluded that he has to do what they're doing. Like a software application, he has tried to define all aspects of life in a few measurable rules–get married, have children, and get old. When Mary came into his life, he tried to apply these rules in their relationship. From day one, he made up his mind to be with her for the rest of his life. Instead of trying to know her better, he tried to act better. He convinced himself that he was in love and worked very hard on pushing that feeling forward.

He realizes that in real life, not all relationships start with absolute love. The stories about love at first sight are just that—stories. When two people get together, they work on their relationship. They make it work and eventually fall in love. That feeling only grows over time. Anthony knew that, and in his mind, he was trying to follow the recipe. Only there's a subtle fact he didn't consider. The want, the effort, the trying, has to be mutual. The love grows, and the relationship hardens only if both sides wish it. It cannot hold if one side is not putting as much work into it as the other. Eventually, that love will fade, and the relationship will fail.

While Anthony was trying to convince himself to love Mary, she was looking for a true love. Instead of trying to understand her and truly see what she was looking for in life, he was immersed in his own misconceptions. No wonder the breakup was so hard on him. He was waking from a delusion and his subconscious was resisting it. He understands all of it now. And it was Kris who made him see the truth. He doesn't say anything and just looks at Kris appreciatively, then stands up, turns around, and walks straight towards Mary's table.

He can see her now. Lovely as ever. But he is looking at her differently. Not a potential wife, nor a savior who brings happiness to his life. But a friend whom he adores so much. A friend who spent time with him and brought some happiness to his life. Mary looks up and sees him. The surprise in her eyes makes Anthony smile. He gets close and says hi.

Mary gets up, hugs him, and says hi. Then she introduces him to Gary. He doesn't seem a bad guy. In fact, Anthony finds no ill will towards him. He has no intention of punching Gary anymore. Anthony explains that he's with his friend, Kris, who noticed her. So, he decided to come over. Mary is pleased to see him. They chat for a short time, and then Anthony returns to his table.

It's as if a heavy load is lifted from his shoulders. He is more content. His appetite seems to be back. As he starts to eat, he looks at Kris and says, "It seems your cheap therapy opened my eyes. I love her alright, but I'm not in love with her. I think subconsciously I knew that, but wasn't ready to accept it."

Kris explains: "Sometimes we plan something in life and expect it to happen. We create a picture-perfect moment of that success. The perfect marriage, perfect spouse, perfect children. It consumes us to the point of delusion. You wanted to get married and start a family so badly that you didn't see Mary as she really is. You convinced yourself that this was your last chance, and you loved her. Granted, you do love her. At least, over time, you started loving her. But you were never in love with her. You were in love with that picture-perfect life. The snapshot of a happy family—the kind of family your parents made."

And then he continues: "But you forgot your father never had a flawless life. He had to work it out with your mother, and the only way they managed to do it was to do it together. They both wanted it to work, and eventually, love grew between them. It's that love that is transferred into your life. You felt that love and warmth and thought this was your last chance to have the same. You forgot to see real life and the real Mary." Kris pauses for a few seconds, then adds, "Maybe what you really ... really ... really, want for this Christmas isn't Mary. Maybe it's happiness and contentment? Or maybe a dose of reality to help you get back on track?"

As Anthony is listening to Kris, he can't help but think that what he is saying is true. In fact, this is something John was trying to tell him. Only he wasn't listening. This confrontation with Mary after three months was the shock he needed to see things more clearly. He is grateful to Kris. He has no idea why he came into his life, how he got hold of his letter, and what his intentions are, but he appreciates what he just did for him.

They finish their meals and return home where Kris had parked his bike next to the building. Before leaving, Anthony reminds him of to-morrow's rehearsal before the party. He comes inside and sits on the sofa. He is still thinking about the whole situation. The future is unclear. Until this afternoon, he had a plan, and it was to get back with Mary. Now things have changed—again. He doesn't have a plan anymore. He's not sure if he'll ever find the right girl, nor if he'll ever have any children.

This is new territory for him. For the first time in his life, he is completely unclear about his future. So, he decides to take Kris and John's advice and leave the future to the future. Que sera, sera!

Christmas Party

The day for the office Christmas party has arrived. Anthony goes to work like every Tuesday. Today he decides to go later than his usual seven thirty. He's planning on some light work–just some emails, a couple of meetings for his project, and later, a mid-morning meeting with Lindsey. By the time these were done, it would be time to head towards the venue for final preparations.

They had invited some of their top clients, so it's important to have everything go without any problems. He meets with his colleagues and reminds them of the Christmas party. Jasmine had sent the invitation to the entire organization two weeks ago. Almost everyone had accepted. This was the first full-fledged party after the shelter-in-place. Everyone was invited to bring their partners. It's going to be a great night. That's what Anthony keeps telling everyone. He goes to see if Lindsey is in, to remind her of the party. She acknowledges it and asks him if everything was going according to their plan. Jasmine and Anthony confirm all is well.

He goes to his desk, takes out his laptop, and starts his work. But first, he's going to have his morning espresso. As he is sipping his coffee and browsing through his emails, he thinks about the night before. No, it wasn't a dream. He actually met Mary for the first time after their breakup and realized his feelings for her were not as deep as he believed them to be. He was pleased with himself for finally facing reality. It wasn't easy.

After lunch, he and Jasmine head to the venue. When they get there, the manager greets them. Anthony relaxes on the couch while Jasmine and the manager go to her office for the last review of the program. He looks around and sees they have decorated the place very nicely. His mind wanders off to the last few weeks. As he is thinking about these events, he realizes that it all started with his letter to Santa and the appearance of Kris, or whatever his name is.

He is amazed at how a simple act like writing a letter led to a chain of events, which led to him becoming cognizant of his feelings. If he hadn't written that letter, he might have been sitting here and still sulking. But he's okay now and he can start the new year fresh. Maybe he will finally find his true love, or maybe he won't. What matters is that today, he is feeling happy. He is beginning to get into the Christmas spirit. His ears are picking up the Christmas songs coming from all corners of the city, and his eyes are feasting on the jolly Christmas decorations in front of the stores on every street. It's a brave new world, and the sky is the limit.

Strangely, he is also grateful for the biker who got hold of his letter. He isn't embarrassed by his letter anymore, nor does Kris' Santa claim bother him. *So what? Let him be Santa.* He smiles at that thought. Speaking of Santa, he wonders if Kris will show up for the party. What if he doesn't? For a moment, he gets worried, then decides that in the worst case, he will play the role of Santa himself. It didn't matter what Kris thought of his performance. He is ready to be Santa. All they need is a Santa costume.

His thoughts don't last long when Kris walks right into the venue. With his usual grin, he greets Anthony, "Hello my boy! How are you feeling today?"

"Much better, thank you. I had an eye-opening moment last night."

"I see! Does this mean you don't love Mary anymore?"

"Oh no, I still care for her, but I'm not in love with her."

"So I gather you don't want me to bring you two together."

Anthony pulls Kris aside and whispers "I don't know what you are anymore. You helped me see the truth about my relationship and I'm grateful for that. But can we skip this Santa business and give me back my letter?"

"Impossible. I still have to deliver your present."

"What present? The deal is over. I don't want to be with Mary anymore." His voice lowers as he continues. "Give me back my letter or I swear I'll do something nasty."

"Ouch! Tough guy, eh? Hold that thought. We have kids to cheer first."

At this moment, Jasmine comes out of the manager's office. Jasmine sees Kris and recognizes him from the zoom meeting. As she gets closer, she smiles and waves at him.

"Hi Kris! So good of you to come."

"Hello my little child. Of course, I would come. Did you expect otherwise?!" he says, winking at her.

"You have your costume with you, I hope."

"Yes, it's in my bag on the bike. I'll go get it."

As Kris goes to get his bag, Anthony asks Jasmine if everything is okay. She assures him that everything is prepared, and they are ready to receive the guests. It's six o'clock, and the invitation was for seven. They have one hour to kill, so they decide to check out Kris' Santa act. This is the last thing they need to do to make sure the evening will go well.

Kris comes in with his bag and Jasmine tells him about the plan and asks him to wear the costume. The venue manager joins them and tells Kris he can use her office as a dressing room. A few minutes later, Kris comes out wearing a Santa costume. He has a false white beard on and is wearing white gloves. He looks like a Santa. He starts walking around, saying, "Ho, ho, ho, Merry Christmas." They all laugh. Now everything is ready. Kris changes back into his regular clothes and they sit at one of the tables, waiting for the guests to arrive. Anthony takes a look at the tables, and sees they are set beautifully. The decorations are all Christmassy. Each table is covered with a white tablecloth and a red one on top of it. At the middle of tables, the centerpieces are consisted of some holly, berries, pine cones and a pillar candle. The centerpieces are slightly different on each table but they all have the same theme. Over the entrance door and around the stage are decorated with garlands made of fir branches. There's a big tree next to the stage where the band will play. The band is already setting up their instruments and checking the sound. There is a dance floor right in front of the band. The open bar is on one side and a couple of bartenders are waiting to serve the guests. Everything is well thought out. *At these prices, they should be well thought out*, Anthony thinks to himself. Anthony turns to Jasmine and says, "Very nice decoration. Good job selecting this place."

"Yes, very fancy-schmancy. A bit too much for my taste." Kris says, then adds, "but I suppose the kids will like it."

"Hopefully the clients, too. We need to make a good impression." She then turns to Kris and asks: "So, Kris, what do you do outside of the Christmas season?"

"Oh, there's plenty to do. The elves and I usually start planning for the next Christmas as soon as this one is done."

Jasmine finds this funny and starts laughing. Anthony is panicking and doesn't know what to say. All he thinks is that he knew something like this would happen.

Kris looks puzzled by Jasmine's reaction as he was sincere in his answer. He turns to Anthony and asks what made her laugh.

Anthony shakes his head and tries to change the subject. "What time is it? I guess the guests are going to arrive shortly."

"Yes, it's almost seven o'clock. We better wait in the reception area to greet them."

They leave the table. Kris heads to the office to be called later. They didn't want the kids to see him just yet. Anthony and Jasmine wait at the reception area. Anthony asks Jasmine if her boyfriend is coming, to which she says yes. Apparently, he was working a bit late and would join later. This prompts Jasmine to ask Anthony how he is coping with his breakup.

"Actually, since last night, I've been feeling much better. I'm not feeling sad anymore."

"Good! I assume you didn't bring a date?"

"No."

"Too soon?" she asks, as they both smile in confirmation.

"I'm okay. There's a lot on my mind right now. I don't think I'm going to get into a new relationship anytime soon." He pauses a couple of seconds, then continues, "You know what, Jas? I'm going to leave it to Fate. If there is someone for me, Fate will bring her into my life."

"Wait a minute, where's Anthony? What have you done to him?" They both laugh again.

"I'm serious!"

"It's not you. You always plan and prepare. This is the first time I'm hearing of you relying on Fate. It's weird!"

"Well, I've tried planning before. Now I'm going to leave it to Fate. Honestly, if nothing happens for me, I'll be quite alright."

"As long as you're happy. It's good to see you cheered. These last four months, you were a complete sour puss."

Both are feeling festive and can hardly wait for the party to start. But the wait is over, and guests start coming in. A few coworkers with their partners at first. Then a couple of clients with their spouses. Lindsey comes in with her husband. They know each other and say hi. Anthony shakes hands with William, Lindsey's husband, and says, "Hey William. Good to see you. Merry Christmas!"

"Tony! How are you? I heard this is all your doing."

"Actually, it's Jas' doing. I just helped here and there."

"Yes, don't you think I didn't notice," Lindsey says.

"It was a team effort. I hope everyone enjoys it," Jasmine interjects.

"I see an open bar. It's definitely going to be an enjoyable night," William says with a grin.

Anthony laughs at his remark. "Well, it's a Christmas party, so enjoy yourselves."

Behind them, the other guests arrive and the party starts getting warmed up. The band has started playing some music. Everyone is mingling and seems to be happy.

Jasmine turns to Anthony and says, "I think it's going to be a good party. People seem to be enjoying themselves." Jasmine looks at the door and sees her boyfriend, James, arriving. James works in a brokerage company as a financial adviser. He had a client to attend to, but he explains their meeting was finished sooner than expected so he could get to the party on time. Jasmine is so happy to see him. Anthony suggests they join the party, and he will greet the rest of the arriving guests.

Anthony is standing at the entrance of the venue waiting for all the guests to arrive. He can see inside the room and the people are having fun. It looks like everyone is there with their partner except him. He ponders on this realization for a bit, and then feels alright. For the first time in a long time, he feels fine being single. In fact, the unknown future and anticipation of moving towards it makes him feel excited. He can't wait to see what is going to happen next in his life. That gives him some courage. He thinks at least he can enjoy this night and leave the future to … well … the future! More guests are arriving, and Anthony greets them and directs them to the room. He is busy with all of this when Kris comes out of the office.

"What are you doing here? People will see you," Anthony says.

"I was bored in there. I'm not a prisoner, you know. Besides, no one will recognize me with the beard and stuff." Kris pauses, looks around, and continues.

"Look at all those hors d'oeuvres. They look yummy on those trays."

Before Anthony can say anything, Kris turns to one of the closest servers who is circling around with a tray, waves at her, and says, "Hey Jennifer, excuse me." The server notices and comes a bit closer.

"What are you doing?" Anthony asks.

"I'm hungry."

The server comes close and asks, "Do you need anything?"

Kris picks up two hands full of appetizers off the tray and says, "Can you bring us some more of these? I haven't eaten since last night."

The server smiles and nods, then returns to the kitchen to fill her tray. Kris' ambush had left only one item on it. Anthony looks angry. He turns to Kris, who is gobbling down the appetizers, and says, "Can you be less conspicuous? Everyone's looking at you."

"Ah, you're imagining things. Have some of these. They taste delicious," Kris says, and extends his hand, filled with food, toward Anthony's face.

"Put your hand down! No thank you, I'll have some later when I go in. Try not to choke on them."

"Pish posh, I can put three of these in my mouth at once and still have room left to tell you that you're getting naughty again," Kris responds as he puts a handful of the appetizers in his mouth. His mouth full of food, he mumbles, "When do the kids arrive?"

"In about half an hour, before dinner is served. We will have the kids on stage. You will come in with presents and spend some time with them. Then everyone will have their dinner and the kids will leave."

"Then I'd better go get ready. When it's time, come and tell me. I'll make an entrance that everyone will love."

"Yeah, make an entrance. Just don't pick a fight with the guests–or the children!!" Kris gives him a dirty look and goes to the manager's office to get ready.

By now, all the guests have arrived, and Anthony joins the party. First, he goes to the open bar and orders a drink. Then he goes to his seat, picking up a couple of hors d'oeuvres on the way. Guests could sit anywhere they liked, but Jasmine had assigned three tables for clients and upper management and a table for themselves next to the VIPs. Anthony takes a seat next to James. He seems to be busy with some food and his drink while looking around and talking to everyone at their table. This may be an opportunity for him to attract some clients. He turns to Anthony and asks, "Tell me, how long to retirement?"

"A long time, and if you try to talk me into buying or selling stocks, I'll punch you." James rolls his eyes. Anthony continues: "I will tell you that Marthia over there may need some advice on her finances. I overheard her this morning asking about financial advice from a colleague. You can pay my commission by shutting up about my finances tonight."

James gives him a side look and fist pumps with him under the table. At this point, Jasmine joins the conversation. "What are you guys up to?"

"Tony is finding me prospects."

"Leave him alone. He has enough problems of his own. Doesn't need you to engage him in finance," Jasmine says.

"Oh yeah, your breakup," James says. "How's it going?"

"My God! Does everyone know about my relationship?" Anthony exclaims.

"You've been grumpy for so long that, yeah, everyone noticed." They both start laughing.

"I'm glad that my misfortune has become the subject of your amusements," Anthony says.

"Okay, seriously, you got lucky. Who needs a relationship?" James says.

Jasmine jumps up and pokes him on his side and says, "Really?! Do you want to get lucky as well?"

James turns to her and says, "I'm just trying to cheer him up, honey. You know you're my life and I can't live one moment without you," he finishes his compliment, then turns to Anthony, shaking his head as if Jasmine can't see. This provokes Jasmine to poke him harder. Anthony is happy and thinks this is a good way to start his holiday. A few more days, and he will have his own bantering with his sisters and maybe even Mom. Dad enjoys it the most when Anthony plays jokes on his mom.

It's eight o'clock and the manager of the charity arrives. Jasmine and Anthony go to welcome her. She informs them that the kids are on the bus waiting to come in. Anthony nods to the master of ceremony, indicating that it's time for the special event. They had practiced it before. He goes on the stage and the band stops playing.

"Ladies and gentlemen," the MC announces. "We hope you are having a good time. Dinner will be served in half an hour. In the meantime, we have a special event prepared for you. Tonight, we have twenty wonderful kids coming here to participate in your party, as well as a special guest who will come in to shower them with presents. You can guess who's coming to town!" Everyone laughs. And he continues: "Do you know who?" And the crowd yells "SANTA!" and begins to cheer.

Looking toward the entrance, he sees the kids in the reception area and he continues: "I'd like to ask you to welcome our very special guests. And also, don't forget to help the charity which has arranged this amazing event. In the spirit of the season, let's be generous and think of others who can't go to grand parties like this."

The children come in and everyone starts clapping as they take the stage. During the announcements, a couple of servers helped set the stage for Santa. This was all planned and rehearsed earlier in the day. While the kids are all on the stage, Anthony signals Kris, who is waiting at the door of the manager's office to come in. Kris is in full Santa costume and as he passes by, Anthony whispers, "Let's see if you can ho, ho, ho," and gives Kris a smirk. Kris passes by without looking at him and just says, "Shut up!" *Yup that's Santa*, Anthony thinks to himself and laughs.

Kris enters the room and starts with a Santa ho, ho, ho. He clearly has charisma, because immediately the crowd is taken with him. Everyone cheers and the children stare at him with dazzled eyes. With his bag of presents, he goes straight onto the stage, sits on the chair which is prepared for him, and calls on the kids to come closer and sit down.

Everyone is quiet and waiting for Santa to work his magic. For the next thirty minutes, Kris talks to the kids, calls them by their names, and asks them to come forward and get their presents. He is quite an entertainer. Anthony can't believe it's the same guy he has been dealing with. The kids are having such a good time, and the guests look amused. In this environment, many people are approaching the charity manager, Mrs. Kelly Hampton, and inquiring how they can contribute to the cause.

As the present giving ceremony ends, they are invited to dinner. Everything is ready. The children sit at the designated tables which are prepared for them, along with the aids, caregivers, and nurses who tend to them. They all seem to be enjoying their meals. The band has started playing some soft background music. Everything is executed to perfection. Anthony can't believe that the party is going so smoothly. Kris has already said goodbye to the kids and left to prepare the toys for other kids around the world so he can deliver them on Christmas Eve. That's what he told the kids and all the guests, anyway. In actuality, he went back to the office to change clothes and leave. Anthony asks him to stay for dinner, but he thinks some kids may recognize him and give away the whole show. With Kris gone, Anthony feels a bit lonely. He thinks Kris did well. He was a true Santa, and the children probably believed him. He didn't seem like a bad person. The only thing that had bothered Anthony since the first day of meeting him was the mystery of how he got hold of his letter. That was the most puzzling and annoying thing about Kris.

I'm going to get that letter back, and get to the bottom of this, he thinks to himself. Strangely, he doesn't feel sad anymore. He's not bothered with time running out to make a family and such. Tonight, he just wants to enjoy the party. He goes back inside and joins the others.

After Party

For celebrities and important people, the after-party is a private extension to the party with a few VIPs. For us mere mortals, the after-party is the day after the party when we go about our business and get on with our lives. This is true for Anthony as well. He wakes up early and prepares for work. Two more days, and he is off for Christmas. His flight is on Friday. He has packed his suitcase and only a few things were left to be added at the last minute. But he still has two more days of work. This is when time runs slow. He turns on his laptop as usual around seven-thirty in the morning.

He's still in the party mood and starts humming one of last night's songs while checking his emails. Not much is going on. People haven't started their work yet. The best thing to do is to get busy with the project and try to wrap it up as quickly as possible. He is deep into his work when an email comes in. He looks at the time and sees it's ten o'clock. Surprised time has gone by so fast; he checks the email. It's from the VP of the department. He is thanking everyone for attending, informing the team that the party was a success, and the clients enjoyed themselves very much. He then thanks Anthony and Jasmine for the great work of planning the party–especially the Santa event. Anthony smiles and is quite pleased with the outcome. He messages Jasmine.

Anthony: "Did you see the email?"

Jasmine: "Yeah! We did great."

Anthony: "Well, you did great. Most of the work was yours."

Jasmine: "It was a team effort. Besides, your friend Kris saved the day. Thanks to you."

Anthony: "Yup, he did good. I think the kids liked him."

Jasmine: "What are you talking about? They loved him. They totally bought he was Santa. Even the guests loved him. I heard from a few people who thought he was the best Santa they had seen. When you see him, please thank him on our behalf."

Anthony: "Sure, will do."

Anthony wonders if he's going to see Kris again. Kris has become a puzzle for him.

It's around noon, and there is a knock on the door. It is Kris. He comes in and Anthony tells him about the email and Jasmine thanking him for doing a great job. Kris seems to be pleased.

"What did you expect? Santa has to do the best Santa act because it's not an act. I was just being myself." Kris says.

"About that. Can we agree not to go down this road again? Enough is enough. You've done a couple of good things, and I am really grateful. But I still don't know what your motive is. I don't even know your real name. Where do you live? Are you a sociopath? Do you plan to kill me before Christmas?"

"I don't know how to convince you I'm Santa anymore. Everything I say, you don't believe me. You have your head stuck in the sand and are not remotely trying to entertain the possibility. So, let's just forget about it. Consider me a stranger who wants to give you the present you asked for."

"We settled this last night. I don't want to be with Mary anymore. It's done."

"Let's change the subject," Kris says. "I came here to take you to lunch."

"Where? Wait a minute. Is this one of your tricks? Is Mary going to be there?"

"Strictly on the level. No Mary and no tricks. Just lunch. We're going to this Mexican place I know. We'll go on my bike."

"In this cold weather? No way I sit in the back of that bike again."

"It's holiday time, and traffic is a killer. The best way to commute is on my bike. So, stop being a sissy, put on your hat and coat, and let's roll."

"Yeah, very Santa like," Anthony says as he puts on his coat, grabs his keys, and follows Kris out the door.

It's windy and Kris is riding his bike like a mad dog. He goes between cars and jumps from one lane to another. Anthony is getting nauseated. He keeps telling him to slow down, but Kris doesn't seem to hear him–or he pretends not to. Finally, they arrive close to the Hudson River. Kris parks his bike close to a food truck, and as they get off the bike, he says, "They have the best Mexican food ever."

"You brought me all this way to a food truck?"

"The food is amazing! The best street tacos you can find. They have this orange sauce which is heavenly."

"Food truck? Twenty minutes in this weather. Food truck?"

"Stop complaining. Eat, then you'll see."

Anthony is still playing his own tune. "Food truck! Meals on wheels. We couldn't go somewhere closer."

Kris orders the food and they find a place to sit. While eating their lunch, Kris asks Anthony, "How are you holding up my boy?"

"Strangely, I'm okay. Looking forward to the two weeks off."

"Now that Mary is out of picture, do you know what you really want for Christmas?"

"Yes! Tell me how you came across my letter, and what exactly is your game?"

"That's not what you want for Christmas."

"How do you know?"

"That's what you want now!" Kris says, and starts laughing loud.

Anthony doesn't think it's funny. "When you first showed up, I didn't know what your motive was. I still don't. Isn't it time to come clean and move on?"

"Are you tired of my company? Or did you not like the food?" Kris asks.

"Amazingly, the food is good. Where do you find these places?"

"Ah, if I tell you, you won't believe it."

"No, I won't, but tell me anyway."

Kris stares hesitantly at Anthony for a moment, then decides to tell him.

"Jose Perez, the guy you see tending to customers – not the one in the back, that's his help."

"What about him?" Anthony asks.

"Hold on to your shirt. I'm telling the story," Kris says. "Last year, his business was struggling. He had this truck for six months, but his business wasn't going anywhere. He also has a six-year-old daughter. She didn't know why her dad was upset all the time, and when she asked her Mom and Dad what was wrong, they would only tell her that people were not buying Dad's food. She knew her father's tacos were very good

because he makes them at home every now and then and they all love it."
Kris picks up another taco and has a bite. While chewing on the food, he
continues.

"So last year when his daughter was five, she wrote her letter to me
with the help of her mother and decided to ask for more people to buy
daddy's food as her present for Christmas."

"Not another Santa story," Anthony says, rolling his eyes.

"I knew you wouldn't believe me."

"That's because you're Santa! You know everything!" Anthony responds sarcastically.

"Shut up and eat your food. I'm telling a story. You asked for it."

"Me and my big mouth."

Kris gives him a sideways look and continues. "So, she writes the letter
and tells me I can see for myself how good Daddy's tacos are, and asks
Jose to make tacos and put it on a plate for me instead of the usual milk
and cookies. Poor man did what she asked to keep her happy. That's how
I found out how good these tacos are. I come here now and then and try
different things. So far, everything has been fantastic."

"The food is really good, but not the story. I was expecting a bit of
truth."

"That was the truth, even if you don't believe it."

"Why did you really bring me here? The Christmas present thing is
done and I'm not buying this Santa stuff."

"I wanted to see how you are doing and to learn what to bring you for
Christmas. Would you like a new girlfriend?"

"What?! What is wrong with you? Are you running a match-making
business? I don't want a girlfriend. I'm okay, thank you very much."

"Okay, okay, no need to snap at me. Come on, I'll take you home. Say
thank you for the great food."

"Thank you."

"Not to me!" Kris barks and looks in Jose's direction. Anthony looks at him and understands, so he goes towards the truck and thanks Jose, and compliments him on the food. Jose looks very happy and asks Anthony to spread the word if he really liked the food. He also points to the website written on the truck and asks him to rate the food if he can. Anthony agrees and heads back towards the bike where Kris is waiting.

"You're going to give him a good rating. He's an honest, hard-working man and I have an obligation to keep bringing people here."

"I thought it was last year's present."

"You think one year of customers is good enough? It has to be continuous until the business picks up. This year she's asked for a puppy."

"And you're going to give her that?"

"Why not? Her parents are okay with it. They wanted to get her a puppy for some time. I can do that and save them a trip to the shelter."

Anthony isn't bothered with his fibs anymore. He jumps on the bike, and they head back home.

It was an interesting lunch. He was happy to have found that place. He's thinking of taking his friends there to surprise them with the new discovery, but now it's time to get back to work. He turns on his laptop and it's business as usual until the afternoon. In the afternoon, when his work is done, he gets up, does a little stretching, and turns on the Christmas tree lights. He then goes to the kitchen to make a cup of cocoa. While making the cocoa, his phone rings. It's his mom. He's a bit worried since there was no reason for her to call, especially since they would see each other in two days. He quickly answers the phone and says, "What's happened?"

"Hello to you, too," his mother says.

"Hi Mom. I was worried something was wrong?"

"Why should anything be wrong? Can't I just call and see how you're doing?"

"Of course you can. It's just a bit unusual. I'll be home in a couple of days. How are you doing? How's Dad?"

"I'm doing good. Thank you for asking. Actually, Dad's the reason I called."

Anthony panics and immediately cuts off his mother before she can continue.

"I knew something was wrong. What has happened? How's Dad? Is it his heart?"

"Tony! Would you let me finish? Dad is okay."

"So, what about him?"

"Do you remember how whenever he comes over there, you take him to that French store and buy him ham?"

"Yes, what about it?"

"He's asking if you can get him a pound of that imported French ham and bring it with you when you come home."

"What? You called me to get you a ham? Where do I shove it? Next to my clothes?! Tell him it's not good for his heart."

"Anthony Emil Russo, shame on you with that dirty mouth. I should wash it out with soap." Then they both start laughing. It's a comment referring to their favorite holiday movie, *A Christmas Story.*

Anthony's middle name is Emil, but he genuinely dislikes it. He was named after his maternal grandfather. Anthony never liked his grandpa. He was a grumpy old man who would always yell at the kids. He often wondered about his grandpa's mean behavior. Maybe the kids behaved badly. But as he grew older, he realized his grandpa was just a bitter old man. Some people never change and are set in their ways. That's why anything out of the ordinary will annoy them. Many times, he thought of dropping his middle name, but after his grandfather's passing, he decided to keep it, even though he prefers not to use it.

Anthony tells his mom instead of bringing the ham, he'll ask the store to deliver. His Mom thinks it won't get there for Christmas, but Anthony promises to pay for urgent delivery. They talk for a bit more and hang up. He knows that the ham thing was an excuse. His parents were worried and wanted to check up on him in their own subtle way. These are the things that make him love them even more. He hasn't told them about his revelation, so they still think he's grieving. He didn't want to talk about it on the phone and decided to tell them about it when he sees them. He calls the store and orders the ham and some other imported goods and asks for a one-day delivery. With the ham business taken care of, now it is time to relax and enjoy this end of autumn afternoon.

It is Thursday, December 21. Anthony wakes up to the sound of rain hitting his window. He looks outside and sees it's still dark from the heavy gray clouds covering the sky. It's a gloomy-looking day, but for Anthony, it makes no difference. He is full of holiday cheer. It is his last day of work and he wants to put it behind him as fast as possible. The best way to do it is to drown himself in it. This way, he won't notice the passage of time. He suddenly craves a walk in the rain. He decides to go to his usual coffee shop and get his coffee from there instead of making it himself. A walk in the rain would be fun.

He puts on his coat, grabs his umbrella, and hits the road. The barista knows him from his patronage through the years, and is pretty surprised at seeing him there on a Thursday. Anthony usually goes to that coffee shop on Tuesdays and some weekends. She greets him and asks what brings him there. Anthony explains he wanted to have a walk in the rain. He then grabs his usual espresso and croissant and goes back to his apartment. It's time to get to work. Fortunately, the day passes with no extraordinary events, no Kris, and no project issues. In the afternoon, he decides to have a relaxing evening. Surprisingly to him, he gets his wish, and the day ends without any problems. That's the way of life. Every dog has its day and today was Anthony's.

Merry Christmas

It's Friday, December 22. Anthony has taken the day off to have enough time to get ready for his flight. He wakes up and goes about his morning routine, then brings his suitcase to add the last-minute items. He has gifts for everyone that need to be gift-wrapped. The check-in suitcase is for all the presents. He's been doing this every year, and sometimes he wonders if even the airport workers know his annual routine. That would be funny.

"No gifts for Dad this year, Mr. Russo?!" He imagines that would freak him out right there and then. The thought makes him smile. He brings the presents out of the closet one by one and puts them on the dining table. He brings the wrapping papers, ribbons, and all the wrapping equipment and sets them on the table. He absolutely despises wrapping gifts, but regardless, he always tries to do the best job he can. After all, it's Christmas, and it comes only once a year, so he tries to make an effort. He gets busy with wrapping, working from the tiniest boxes to the big ones. He wraps each one with care and precision. Finally, around noon, after taking many breaks in between and wasting a lot of paper, ribbon, and cards, he is done. All the presents are stacked up on the other side of

the table and they look pretty. The whole scene looks very Christmassy. He is hoping that all the boxes will fit in his extra-large suitcase. He has a big suitcase he bought years ago just for this occasion.

It's noon, and he's hungry. He suddenly remembers the taco place where Kris took him. He then realizes Kris hasn't been around for the past few days. He hasn't seen him since the party. His mind starts wandering. *What is he up to now? It doesn't matter anymore,* he thinks, because in a few hours he's going home, and by the time he gets back, Christmas will be over. Santa or not, he has to go away and there'll be no more talk of the letter or the gift. The thought of it gives him a sense of relief. He survived this crazy stranger. Although he admits Kris has been a big help in the realization of his inner feelings towards Mary, he is looking at life from a new angle. One that doesn't put too much pressure on him to get married. One that lets life take its course. Of course, he would still plan on some things, but dating will be paused until after the New Year. Immediately, he has a new idea. What if he waited until his birthday before dating again? Not that his previous brilliant idea went so well. No more revelations. He goes into the kitchen to see what he can find to eat. He hasn't been cooking lately—not even scrambled eggs. He puts on his coat, picks up his wallet, and goes out for a nice walk and a good meal. Maybe he'll go to the Greek café two blocks away. Gyro followed by a rich Greek coffee seems to be a good idea.

The flight is around six o'clock in the afternoon. He still has some time to spend. Usually, he takes a twenty-minute power nap before heading to the airport. It gives him the energy to deal with security lines, bag checks, and all. There was a time when flying used to be a happy event and people would look forward to going to the airports. Nowadays it's just standing in lines and waiting in uncomfortable chairs. It's smart to be prepared for all kinds of strange eventualities. Anthony prefers road trips to flying, but they take a lot of time, and during the winter, the roads are dangerous and unpredictable. To be honest, during the holidays, flight schedules are not so on time, but at least the airports are warm and there is plenty of room to roam around.

He still has a couple of hours to kill. As he's going through his bags to make sure nothing is missed, there's a text notification on his phone. It's Kris. He is puzzled, because in all the time they've been together, he never gave Kris his phone number. Maybe he got it from the directory.

Kris: *"Today's the big day. Going home?"*

Anthony: *"Yup."*

Kris: *"Have fun and enjoy your holiday."*

Anthony: *"You too."*

Kris: *"So what is it going to be for your present?"*

Anthony: *"Can we not do this now? Certainly, no Mary."*

Kris: *"Are you happy with that decision?"*

Anthony: *"Yes. I am happy. In fact, I haven't felt this calm and happy for the past few months."*

Kris: *"Then what am I going to give you? Do you want a Ring for your door?"*

Anthony: *"No, have one."*

Kris: *"You can give it to your parents."*

Anthony: *"They've got one."*

Kris: *"How about an iPad?"*

Anthony: *"You make iPads? Isn't that copyright infringement?"*

Kris: *"I don't make them. I have a contract with Apple. I have contracts with all the major manufacturers. They provide me with the goods."*

Anthony is developing a liking for these creative responses from Kris. He's wondering how far Kris will go with his fibs. So, he continues.

"Really!? How do they make money if they give you all these goods for free?"

Kris: "Through royalty fees from the money we make out of advertisements and charity organizations."

Anthony: "Very good! So, you're running a business. What happened to the good will to mankind and helping the poor?"

Kris: "What happened to paying bills and eating?"

Anthony: "I thought the amount of milk and cookies you consume in one night will cover you for a whole year."

Kris: "What do you think I am, a bear? I also have bills to pay. Running the toy business needs money."

Kris continues: "Okay, I'll leave you to your power nap. Have a great time."

Anthony is puzzled again by the amount of personal information Kris knows about him. But he's used to it and thinks nothing of it.

The flight is on time and after three hours, Anthony finds himself in front of his parents' home. He feels relieved. He waits before going in, just wanting to absorb the moment. He stands in front of the house and looks at the decorations. It's like every year. The big Santa on the porch, reindeer on the front lawn, multicolored lights are all around the house. Mom has hung the wreath on the front door. Everything looks pretty, and it reminds him of his childhood. At the same time Anthony was reminiscing, Mom was pacing from kitchen to living room, every now and then looking outside, waiting for his arrival. She sees him standing there and goes to the door. She opens the door and Anthony rushes towards her, and showers her with hugs and kisses.

"What are doing standing outside? It's cold. You don't want to catch a cold right before Christmas."

"I was admiring the outside decorations."

"It's the same as every year."

"Good. I like that."

They go inside. The fire is on, and the house feels warm. Mom has been baking cookies, and the smell of fresh cookies is everywhere. While they go to the family room, Anthony sniffs a bit and asks, "Fresh cookies?" Mom replies with a smile: "Of course!" Dad comes into the room. He was in his study reading the funnies on the internet. Dad is a fan of newspaper comic strips, among them Andy Capp, Garfield, Peanuts, and Beetle Bailey. Every day he goes to his computer and reads a few online. He hugs his son and welcomes him home.

"I ordered your ham. Did it arrive?"

"Not yet. Maybe tomorrow," his father says.

"Did you read all your comic strips for the day?"

Dad laughs and says, "Yes. Andy was up to his no-good mishaps." They both laugh while his mother shakes her head.

"Have you eaten?" his mother asks.

"Yes, Mom."

"Then go unpack while I make some hot cocoa. You can have it with cookies."

"Snickerdoodle?"

"Yes."

"Yippee. I won't be long."

While going upstairs to unpack his suitcases, Amber comes down.

"Hey big brother. Your flight was on time!"

"Did you just get home?"

"Yes. Our flight was delayed. Is mom making hot cocoa?" she asks.

"U huh. I'm having some with my snickerdoodles."

"How can you prefer that to chocolate chips?"

Anthony sticks his tongue out at his sister and goes upstairs to his room. Amber starts laughing and goes down to join Dad in the family room.

Anthony unpacks and takes a quick warm shower. He has his Christmas pajamas on. They are red and have Santa riding on his sleigh all over them. There are some elves here and there. They're very Christmassy. Now that he's home, he is completely in Christmas mode.

"You wore your Christmas pajamas already?" Amber asks as he comes downstairs.

"Yeah, why aren't you wearing yours?"

"I was so tired I forgot. Tomorrow night," she says with a smile.

While they're having their hot cocoas and cookies, Dad asks Anthony how he's been.

"I'm actually pretty okay," Anthony answers. "I know I was down at Thanksgiving, but now I feel fine."

They are relieved to see him feeling himself again. Amber is curious to know more and asks, "What changed? Are you two getting back together?"

"Oh, no. I just realized I wasn't in love with Mary. It was all in my head."

"You mean you don't love her anymore?"

"No, it's not that. I still care for her deeply. But I realized I was forcing myself into believing I was in love with her because I just wanted to start a family."

"Having a family is a good thing. Don't you want that anymore?"

"I want it, but I'm not going to let those wishes consume me anymore. If it happens, better. If not, so be it. I'm not going to obsess about it."

"Obsessing about anything is bad. Try not to obsess about it, son," his father says, leaning towards Anthony, who is sitting on the floor next to him, and pats him on his back a couple of times. Mom and Amber start laughing. Anthony joins in. They drink their cocoa and help Mom clean up, then everyone goes to their rooms to sleep.

The next morning, Anthony joins his parents and sister in the kitchen for breakfast. He had a good night's sleep and feels energized. He asks Mom if she needs his help with anything. She gives him a shopping list to get some last-minute items for Christmas Eve. Usually, they have a family meal on Christmas Eve. On Christmas Day they open their presents, have breakfast, and then try to have a relaxing day. Anna and Walter will join them for Christmas Eve dinner and the Christmas Day gift exchange. Anthony takes his father's car and drives to the store. On the way, he texts his friend, John.

Anthony: "Hey, I'm here. We'll see each other the day after Christmas?"

John: "You're coming to our house. Bibi wants to see you."

Anthony: "We were supposed to go out with the guys."

John: "They'll be here too. It was going to be a surprise. I'll cook."

Anthony: "You cook! That is a surprise."

John: "Dear Tony, p-off, signed John."

Anthony laughs at that text and writes back.

"Okay will be there. Hi to Bibi and kids."

John: "Just did. They send their love. See you."

He starts the car and goes shopping. When he gets back, everyone is busy cleaning up and making preparations. Anthony's a bit surprised. It's just the family, and he wonders why all the commotion. He goes to the kitchen, puts the bags on the island counter, and asks Mom if they're having a big party or something. Mom confirms and says, "We wanted to keep it a surprise for the last minute. Your aunt Jane is coming for dinner tomorrow night."

Anthony has a maternal aunt who lives in town. He knows his grandma joins them for Christmas Eve every other year. Every year, one of her daughters invites her for Christmas Eve dinner and this year it was Aunt Jane's turn. But apparently, they'll be joining them, and that means that Grandma will also be coming. Anthony is almost jumping up for joy and says, "I love Aunt Jane. So, Grams will be coming too."

"Yes, this year they'll all be here with us. Not only will they be coming, but Sammy and his wife, and Sally, with her husband and kids, will be coming too." They are Aunt Jane's children and Anthony's cousins. Anthony is delighted with the news.

"So, Dad made up with Uncle Bill?" Amber and Mom start laughing and Mom nods in confirmation.

"They made up after Thanksgiving," she says.

Dad joins the conversation angrily: "Under duress. Otherwise, I wouldn't talk to that arrogant egomaniac who thinks of no one but himself."

Anthony's father, Luca and Uncle Bill don't really like each other, and they find any excuse to get into an argument and stop talking. It's hard to believe, but their latest escapade was over the NFL. Uncle Bill cheers for the Chiefs, while Luca is a Browns fan. Luca insists fans should cheer for their own state's team, even if they're not champions. Uncle Bill probably cheers for the Chiefs to spite him. Whatever the reason, it caused another friction between them. But since Anthony was upset over his breakup, Mom and Aunt Jane gave their husbands an ultimatum to make up so that the whole family can gather for Christmas Eve. They didn't know that Anthony was over his breakup and feeling much better. Anthony realizes it was probably a good idea he didn't talk about his revelation sooner, or Aunt Jane's family wouldn't be joining them. Especially since that meant that grandma would also be there.

"Good. I don't know why you don't like Uncle Bill. He's always been very nice to us."

"That's his act. He wants to show what a good person he is. Believe me, he isn't."

"This feud between you two must have a cause. What started it Dad?"

"Jane and me," Mom answers. "Each son-in-law wanted to be the favorite with Grams and Pops. You kids weren't born yet when these two went into competition with each other and it's never stopped."

"So, who became the favorite?" Amber asks.

"Neither. My father hated both of them," Mom answers.

"Pops hated everyone. God bless his soul," Anthony adds. Everyone laughs.

"Then why did they continue their rivalry?" Amber says.

"Because, dear, men are idiots. Your dad and Uncle Bill included."

Dad is not amused at Mom's comment and gives her a dirty look, which she completely ignores. Teasingly, Amber asks, "Tony too?"

"Oh no. My Tony is an exception. I don't know how he turned out to be so smart."

Dad is bewildered and says, "Wha...? Yeah, Tony is the only man in the world who is not an idiot. The rest of us are beneath his royal highness."

"Momma's boy!" Amber teases and she and Dad start laughing hard. Anthony looks at them with anger and then turns to his mom and says, "Why do you give them an excuse?"

Mom goes towards him, pinches both his cheeks, gives him a kiss on one cheek, and says, "Don't listen to them, dear. They're just jealous."

Anthony shakes his head and Dad and Amber laugh even harder. The rest of the day, they prepare everything for the Christmas Eve party. Anthony is thrilled to have Aunt Jane's family with them. He likes both Sally and Sammy. They had wonderful times together as kids.

It's the day of Christmas Eve. Everyone is excited. The family wakes up and has breakfast and they go about their business. There's not much left to do except wait for the guests who will arrive in the afternoon. Anthony asks Amber if she would like to drive around the town to see the Christmas decorations. She agrees to go. They take Dad's car and go for a drive.

In the car, Anthony asks his sister, "So, how are you doing? How's residency?"

"Very hard, but good."

"You mean to tell me that you can now cure diseases? You're a full doctor?"

"I don't have a lot of experience. Ergo residency. But yes, I can diagnose diseases and cure them."

"Wow! My little sister—a real doctor. I never thought you'd be that smart."

"Why? What's wrong with me?"

"You forgot? Your math was horrible, and you had ADHD. You were a complete idiot," Anthony laughs.

"Shut up. I was not."

"What is your plan after residency?"

"I have to find a job in a hospital or a clinic."

"No office of your own?"

"I have neither the experience nor the money to open an office of my own. I need to work in a good hospital for a few years to gain that experience."

"Are you going to come back home, or do you prefer staying in LA?"

"For now, I think I'll stay there."

"I see! So, I can assume that there is a guy involved."

Amber blushes and says, "Shut up!"

"Oh, there is a guy! Tell me about him. Is he a good boy? If he puts one foot wrong, I'll come and punch him in the nose."

"He's okay. I didn't want to say anything yet because it's too soon. I was planning to introduce him to Mom and Dad sometime next year."

"As long as you're happy."

They drive around the town and stop for some coffee before they drive back home.

It's the afternoon of Christmas Eve. Before the guests arrive, the dinner table is set and everything is ready. All four of them are sitting in the living room. The first people to arrive are Anna and Walter. They came before the others to spend some family time together. They hug and kiss and sit in the family room. Mom asks the kids to bring the presents in and put them all under the tree. They do and now the tree looks fantastic. The trimmings are beautiful, and the presents give the tree an impressive look. Eventually, Aunt Jane's family arrives. It's a bustle. Everyone hugs everyone. Kisses are in the air. You can see lipstick traces on almost everyone's cheek.

Grams enters the house and the children jump all over her. For an eighty-year-old woman, she looks pretty fit. Anthony remembers to tell her that. She is pleased to hear it. They also have brought their own presents, and they all go under the tree. Sammy and his wife Julia don't have any children yet. But Sally has a twelve-year-old son, Jacob. He's Gram's first great-grandson, and she is very happy about it. Dad is finally talking to Uncle Bill. When he gets inside, Anthony goes to him, shakes his hand, and then hugs him and says, "Hi Uncle Bill. Good to see you, man. You look great!"

"Tony!! How are you, dear boy? Thank you, I work out, you know. I try to keep myself fit," Uncle Bill says.

"Good for you." Then he turns to his aunt and says,

"Aunt Jane, it's good to see you here. How are you doing?"

Aunt Jane grabs him and gives him a big kiss and says, "Hi baby. It's good to see you too. I'm very good. It's Christmas Eve. What could be better?"

"That's why you're my favorite aunt. You *get* Christmas."

"I'm your only aunt, you naughty boy," she says, as they both break into laughter.

The greetings are completed and they all go to the living room. Everyone finds a place to sit, and Dad offers drinks. Soon everyone has a drink in their hand and are talking to each other. The conversations go from reminiscence of memories to gossip and hearsay about other relatives. The room warms from the crowd, and Anthony decides to get some fresh air before dinner. He slips out and goes outside on the porch.

It's dark and the street is almost empty. People seem to be inside their homes celebrating Christmas Eve. It's started to snow. The snowflakes dance their way to the ground under the street lights. Anthony is filled with joy. Snow on Christmas Eve – it couldn't get any better. Through the living room window, he can see inside. His family and relatives are there talking and laughing. For Anthony, it is such a great scene. He is grateful that everyone is there. He turns to the street and stares at the snow falling down. Suddenly, from the corner of the front lawn, someone calls him. He turns his head to see who's there. It's Kris leaning back on his Harley!

"Hello Tony!" Kris says with a loud voice. He looks cheery and has his usual wide grin. Anthony is completely shocked to see him there. He didn't hear the bike or see him approach. He doesn't know where Kris came from.

Anthony walks towards Kris and says, "What are you doing here? How did you find my home address? Wait a minute. Did you ride your bike all the way here in this weather?"

"Did you think I would forget you? I still have your present to deliver."

"Will you leave me alone? There is no present."

"On the contrary, there is. It's Christmas Eve, my son, and I shall deliver what you want for Christmas."

Before Anthony can say anything, something extraordinary happens. Right in front of his eyes, Kris changes into someone else. A bright light appears and he morphs into a different person as if someone else just stepped outside the light. His bike transforms into a sleigh and there are reindeer attached to it. In an instant, Kris turns into an older man–probably in his sixties, wearing Santa clothes. He is a bit shorter than Kris and his beard is fuller and all white. He is slightly fuller than Kris. He wears a darker red costume. A bit brighter than burgundy, but the clothes are made from silk and suede. There is fur all around his sleeves, at the bottom of his coat, and on his boots. The fur is bright white and looks so fluffy that the slightest movement of air makes it twirl. His boots are soft leather. It's as if a designer has made them. They're very chic. His belt is of the same soft leather and matches the boots and has a silver buckle. His coat has silver buttons which match the buckle of the belt. He is wearing a Santa hat, one of those stocking cap style winter hats. The hat also has fur around it and a pom-pom on top made of the same fur. He also has no tattoos.

The sleigh is a work of art. A magnificent piece of workmanship. It's simple yet elegant. The reindeer seem restless. They're stumping their hoofs and snorting. Misty clouds are coming out of their noses with every exhale. There's an aura of soft white color surrounding all of them, as if they're glowing. Everything looks surreal, especially under the falling snow. Anthony is speechless. It's a picturesque scene he is witnessing. His jaw drops. It really is Santa Claus. He gazes at Santa and with innocent excitement says, "You are real!" He pauses a moment, then cautiously asks, "Are you real?"

Santa, in a jolly tone, replies, "Well, of course, my son. I'm as real as real gets." Then, in a sneaky tone, he asks, "Did you ever doubt me?"

Anthony doesn't know what to say, and gets embarrassed remembering his doubts. But here he is, standing right in front of the big man himself. He can't believe it. Without thinking, he blurts out, "Are M&M's real?"

"I hope not, otherwise I'll pass out right here," Santa answers with a wink.

Anthony realizes what he just said and smiles.

"Then why the disguise, sir? Why didn't you come to me as yourself?"

"That's part of the plan. If I had shown up as myself, it wouldn't have the same impression on you. You needed someone outside your comfort zone to guide you through your true feelings." Then, grinning mischievously, he adds, "Besides, I also like to get a kick out of it."

"But ... why me?" Anthony asks.

"Because you wrote to me!"

"I didn't get back with Mary, so what was the point?"

"Do you remember when you were a kid, and you always asked me for what you really ... really ... really wanted?"

"Yes."

"Is getting back with Mary what you really ... really .... really want?"

Anthony pauses a moment and then says, "No, not really. Now that I know how I feel."

"Then what is it you really ... really ... really want for Christmas?"

Again, Anthony pauses. He looks around, then looks inside the house. The family is still in the living room. They are completely oblivious to the things that are happening out here and are laughing and talking. Anthony thinks for a moment and says, "To be happy. To be content and not feel sorrow for my breakup. And to be healthy and have my family surrounding me. To have my grams with us." He points to the window and the people inside and says, "This."

"And do you have it?"

"Yes." Anthony replies with a smile.

"Did I bring you the right present?" Santa asks.

Anthony suddenly realizes that without Kris' mischievousness, he wouldn't understand his true feelings and might not even have come home for Christmas. He wouldn't have this joy in his heart. Kris was the source of it all. He comes to realize that Santa, in all actuality, helped him to get what he really ... really ... really wants for Christmas.

"Oh yes, sir," he answers. "You did." Smiling in satisfaction, he continues. "Thank you for helping me to see the truth about my relationship. Thank you, Santa." His eyes are moist, and he feels a deep joy in his heart. At this moment, Anthony is feeling he's the happiest man in the world.

"You're welcome, my boy. Why don't you go in and spend some time with your loved ones? I have to deliver presents now." Santa smiles at him, and Anthony thinks his smile is the warmest he has ever seen. He still cannot believe all this is happening. Santa climbs onto his sleigh and the reindeer are ready to take off, when suddenly he remembers something. He turns to Anthony and says, "Can you do me a favor?"

"Anything, sir. By the way, I am very sorry for behaving badly with you, Kris ... um ... both of you?!"

Santa laughs out loud and says, "Think nothing of it. It's part of the job."

"Sorry I didn't believe in you, Santa."

"For some people, seeing is believing. Some don't need to see to believe, and there are some who decide not to believe, even when they see it. I'm glad you're not one of the latter group." Then he leans forward and continues, "You're not, are you?"

"Oh no sir, I completely believe in you now," Anthony immediately responds.

"Good." Santa says before bending down to grab a small, gift-wrapped box. He hands it over to Anthony and says, "There's been a mishap in gift delivery. I'm getting old and can't keep up with it all, you know." Anthony smiles as Santa continues.

"After you return to New York, will you kindly deliver this to Mr. Thompson, who runs a deli near your office? He's a couple of blocks away. The address is on the box. You have to be there on January 9. It's a Tuesday–the same day you go into the office, so it won't be too far."

There's a small gift card attached to it. On one side it reads *Mr. Thompson* and on the other is the address. Anthony accepts the box and agrees to deliver it. But he's curious why so long after Christmas and asks, "Won't it be too late for Christmas?"

"Mr. Thompson returns from his vacation on the eighth and will be in the store the day after." Santa replies. "Oh, one more thing. You have to be there at one o'clock in the afternoon. He's going to be there at that time. Can you do it?"

"Yes sir. I promise."

"Exactly one in the afternoon. Don't forget."

This request puzzled Anthony, but who's going to argue with Santa? He reassures him he will do it to the letter, as requested. Santa grabs the bridle, adjusts himself in the sleigh then says, "Don't forget to be good, Tony. And when you get a chance, write to me from time to time. I'd like to know how you're doing." After that, in a deep voice, yells, "Merry Christmas my boy! Ho ... Ho ... Ho." He pulls on the bridle, and at the same time, calls out to the reindeer to climb.

"On Dasher, on Prancer ..." With that, the reindeer start to ascend quickly. In the blink of an eye, they are halfway in the sky, leaving a trail of sparkling stars. Anthony stares up at the sky until they disappear. He looks around and sees no one. He then looks inside, and they also don't seem to have noticed all that noise and commotion. His Mom appears at the door and asks, "Tony, what are you doing out here in the cold?"

Anthony looks up again and there's no trace of Santa or his sleigh.

"Did you notice anything unusual here?" he asks his mother.

"When?"

"Right now, like a minute ago."

"No, what happened? Was there an accident?"

"No, nothing like that. Doesn't matter."

"We're ready to sit down for dinner. Come on in before you catch a cold."

"Let's go," Anthony says as he walks to his mother and they go inside.

For Anthony, this was a once-in-a-lifetime experience. He couldn't believe that Santa Claus himself had visited him. Inside the house, everyone was at the dinner table. Anthony joins them and they spend the best Christmas Eve he can remember. On Christmas Day, they wake up and have breakfast. Anna and Walter come in early to take part in the gift exchange. Everyone opens their presents and is excited about receiving such delightful gifts. Later in the day, they all watch a Christmas movie, then reminisce on that Christmas when they bought a tree they couldn't afford, and laugh. Anna says she still remembers the poor man's face when Dad gave him the kiss. The day after Christmas, Anthony goes to John's house as planned. He meets with his friends and their families. This is one of the best Christmases he can remember.

After Christmas comes New Year. The family celebrates the change of the year together. They drink champagne and sing *Auld Lang Syne*. Anthony's resolution is to leave the future to the future and not to worry too much about meeting his soulmate and making a family. And then it is time to go back to his life in New York. Vacation is over until next year. He says goodbye to his family, grabs his suitcases, and heads back to New York.

Conclusion, give or take

It's January 9. With the sound of the alarm, Anthony wakes up. Today is an office day, so he skips making coffee. He's about to go out when he remembers Santa's box for Mr. Thompson. For a moment, he hesitates to take it with him. He's thinking it's too late to give Christmas presents. Then he remembers he promised the big man, and how he said he believed in him. If that's what Santa wants him to do, then that's what he's going to do. He grabs the box from the drawer, puts it in his coat pocket and goes to the office. As usual, he buys his espresso and croissant from the coffee shop. The past week has been very productive. Anthony has managed to deliver the first part of the software. His team has been working on it full-time. He's very proud of his team's achievement. Around mid-day, Lindsey pulls him aside.

"Let's go in that room and talk," she says, pointing to a meeting room nearby.

"What's up?" Anthony asks. "Am I being fired?"

"Maybe. In a way. Let's talk about it."

Now Anthony is getting worried. They go inside the meeting room and close the door. Lindsey begins the conversation.

"You know how important this project is in the way we do our business," she begins.

"Yes. And my team has provided Stage One successfully."

"This is a high-profile project, Tony, and it has visibility all the way up to the CEO."

"Okay. Did I do something wrong?"

"Well, technically, I have to fire you from your position."

"I don't understand. What do you mean, technically?"

"I mean, you won't be our senior software engineer anymore."

Anthony is upset. He doesn't understand what has gone wrong. He can't think straight. The only thing that comes into his mind is "why?"

Lindsey continues. "Because you have been promoted to manager of the AI department."

Anthony doesn't get it at first, but then he begins to absorb the news. They have promoted him. Now he is getting angry at Lindsey for leading him on to believe he's getting fired.

"What kind of message delivery is this? You scared me. If this is your way of giving good news, how will you give the bad news?"

Lindsey begins to laugh and says, "I had requested a promotion for you, and they sent me the memo this morning. This delivery has made a lot of noise in the company and they're very pleased with your performance. The request for promotion was immediately approved. You will still report to me, but you will also have your own AI department to run. Your salary will also increase along with your bonuses." She hands him the approval letter. Anthony reads it and is very pleased with everything.

"How is it? Are you happy?" she asks.

"Yes. Thank you for the promotion. So, technically, you did fire me from my previous position."

Lindsey laughs again, agrees, and Anthony smiles.

As they leave the meeting room, Anthony realizes that his responsibilities have increased, and he'd better set aside his personal problems for a while, until he is settled into this new position. He goes back to his desk and looks at his watch. It's ten minutes to one. Suddenly, he remembers the box. He decides he can have his lunch while he's out delivering the present. He grabs his coat, checks the pocket to make sure the box is still there, turns off his laptop, and goes to the deli. The address is on the box. He knows where it is. It's just a couple of blocks away. He can be there in ten minutes. He's walking fast to make sure he'll get there at one o'clock. After all, he doesn't want to get on Santa's naughty list. Anthony sees the deli and looks at his watch. It's a couple of minutes to one. He's made it. As he rushes towards the door, a lady reaches the door at the same time. They pause at the door for a second to let the other in. Anthony looks at her and suddenly feels like the gates to heaven have opened and an angel has appeared. He is speechless. His heart starts pounding in his mouth. He can barely breathe. He hasn't seen such beauty before. The woman is about his own age. She is brunette with hair that comes to her shoulders. She's wearing a light grey business dress with a red wool coat on top and soft leather gloves the same color of her coat. It looks very fashionable. For a moment, they exchange looks and gaze into each other's eyes. Time has stopped for Anthony and he's wishing it will remain still forever. He doesn't want this moment to end.

He catches his breath and says, "Oh sorry, you go first."

The lady blushes and says, "It's okay, you seem to be in a hurry. You first."

They stand there and neither one moves. Anthony cannot take his eyes off this lady. He suddenly comes to himself and realizes he's been staring at her.

"Hi ... I'm Tony."

"Hi Tony, I'm Stella."

"Stella, as in Kowalski?" he asks with a smile.

"My parents were big fans of Marlon Brando."

Anthony smiles too and thinks she has the cutest smile. He is beginning to understand what love at first sight means. He feels head over heels for Stella. He barely composes himself and asks her to go in first. His manner impresses Stella. She enters the deli and Anthony follows her. She turns to Anthony and says, "I usually come here to have lunch around this time, but I haven't seen you here before."

"I've never been here. My friend asked me to deliver something to the owner. I think I'll try the food."

"They have great sandwiches."

They approach the man behind the counter. It appears to be Mr. Thompson. Anthony turns to Stella and asks, "What are you having?"

Stella gently holds Anthony's arm and says: "Chicken sandwich with Swiss on rye. That's my favorite."

Anthony is beaming inside and says, "Then I'll try that one." He turns to Mr. Thompson.

"Two chicken sandwiches with Swiss on Rye."

He asks Stella to allow him to treat her to the sandwich. She thanks him and agrees on the condition that next time it will be her treat. Anthony agrees and thinks, *wow there's going to be a next time.* As he pays for the sandwiches, he turns to the man behind the counter and asks, "Are you Mr. Thompson?"

"Yes," the man answers.

Anthony takes out the box, hands it over to him, and says, "A friend asked me to give this to you."

Mr. Thompson looks at the box and opens it. Inside is a key. He smiles and understands. He puts the key in his pocket, then, from one of the drawers under his register, takes out an envelope and gives it to Anthony. Anthony is puzzled.

"What's this?" he asks.

"I don't know. It's yours. I mean, it belongs to whoever brings the key."

"A few weeks back, I was going on vacation. A friend of mine recommended subletting my apartment to this biker who was in town for a few weeks on business," Mr. Thompson explains.

"This biker... he had a beard, tattoos all over his body, and on his knuckles had 'fist on me' tattooed?" Anthony asks, beginning to understand.

Mr. Thompson is glad that Anthony recognized him and says, "Yeah, that's the guy. Rough. And a bit scary."

"Tell me about it," Anthony says.

"Anyway, he leaves and informs me he'll send the key with a guy and I should give him the envelope. I thought he would be trouble, but the poor guy had fixed my stove and painted my bedroom before leaving. Goes to show you can't judge people by their looks."

"You sure can't." Anthony holds up the envelope and says thanks to Mr. Thompson. Stella looks perplexed and amused by the whole story.

"You knew the guy?"

"Yes, he's the one who gave me the box to deliver." He is curious to know what's in the envelope. He looks at the envelope and opens it. Inside is an elegant card. On the card, in beautiful handwriting, is written: "Sorry for the delay. Couldn't be helped. S." He looks at Stella and she looks back and smiles.

"I'm a software engineer. I work at a company a couple of blocks away."

"I work in sales. Our office is right around the corner."

"Do you think it's possible to have another meal together? Let's say tonight?"

"It's possible, but not tonight."

"I'll give you my number. You call me when we can set a time for the possibility."

"Hmmm ... a bit cheesy, but we'll work on that."

Their sandwiches are ready. Stella thanks him again and leaves. Anthony heads back to the office. As he's walking back, he thinks of what happened and is completely confused. When he was planning on having a family, it didn't work out. When he decided not to look for it, this angel arrives right from heaven. He was supposed to give dating a rest for a while. How did this happen? Santa put his soulmate in his path right when he decided to slow down. That was his gift to Anthony. As I said before—sometimes Fate has other plans which usually don't go with our plans.

Have a very Merry Christmas!